The Appeal

A NOVEL BY

Jerzy Andrzejewski

The Appeal

Translated by Celina Wieniewska
with a preface by Jan Kott

The Bobbs-Merrill Company, Inc.
Indianapolis · New York

also by Jerzy Andrzejewski

The Inquisitors
The Gates of Paradise
Ashes and Diamonds
He Cometh Leaping Upon the Mountains

THE BOBBS-MERRILL COMPANY, INC.
A Subsidiary of Howard W. Sams & Co., Inc.
Publishers/Indianapolis • New York • Kansas City

Preface

THE APPEAL – Jerzy Andrzejewski's latest book – was
written in Poland, but has never been published there. It
belongs to the emigré literature of writers who are not
emigrés and remain in their countries. As in the case of
works by Daniel and Sinyavski or the great novels by Solshenitsin, the 'emigrés' are the manuscripts which had
crossed frontiers and have been published in places where
there is no censorship.

An *Appeal*, but to whom? The title of the novel is Kafka-
esque. Joseph K. of *The Trial* tries in vain to find a Court
of Appeal in which he could prove his innocence. He is
guilty, because he had been born. This is quite sufficient.
In Eastern Europe, Kafka seems to be a much more realist
writer than in the West. You are guilty, because you were
born a Pole, a Jew, a Czech, a Ukrainian or a Tartar.
You are even guilty if you were born a Russian. You are
guilty because you are a citizen. In the eyes of the Party
or the State you are guilty always.

In Warsaw, in the very centre of the city, where Jeru-
salem Avenue intersects New World Street, quite near
Three Crosses Square, a very large building, rebuilt after
the war, houses the Central Committee of the United

Workers' Party. The various wings are built around three or four courtyards and contain endless corridors and passages. In order to get into the building, you need a pass which is then checked and rechecked in each courtyard and every corridor. The people of Warsaw call this structure ' The Edifice '. In this Kafka-esque ' Castle ' the First Secretary of the Party occupies offices on one of the upper floors.

It is to him that the protagonist of Andrzejewski's novel, Marian Konieczny, addresses his appeal. The name seems significant; in Polish it means ' necessary ', or, by extension, ' inevitable ', ' indispensable ', ' requisite '. Like Joseph K. in Kafka's *Trial,* Marian K. stubbornly insists that he is innocent. Justice is somewhere high up, both the Divine and the Communist kind. Marian Konieczny believes unshakeably in both. ' Thanks be to you, God Almighty,' he concludes his appeal, ' for having heard my prayers and thanks be to you, Citizen First Secretary. From the depths of my heart I thank you and promise you solemnly that I shall strive with all my strength to serve selflessly and efficiently People's Poland and the New Order, and may this come to pass in the name of the Father, the Son and the Holy Ghost, Amen.'

Marian Konieczny is guilty because he was born in the middle twenties in the north-eastern frontier area of Poland. He was arrested for the first time by the Gestapo when he was seventeen, for the second time – by the Polish Security Police when he was twenty-two, for the third time on the instructions of an ordinary public prosecutor when he was thirty-one. He was arrested by the German occupants for having hidden arms belonging to his elder brother who was active in the Resistance. For three months he had been beaten on his legs, brought round by cold water being poured on him, then beaten again. He did not talk. He was arrested by the Polish Security Police for lack of revolutionary vigilance. He had been the commandant of a Citizens' Militia post. The girl with whom he lived and whom he wanted to marry had brothers who had gone away from home and whose whereabouts were unknown to the family. Unexpectedly, one of them was captured with arms in his hand when a forest gang was being liquidated. He was condemned to death, but not before Konieczny's arrest. During investigation, a Security lieutenant persuaded Konieczny that ' objective ' truth and his own good required him to accuse the girl of having maintained contact with her brothers. Konieczny signed the statement in accordance with ' the conditions of the class struggle ' and got a sentence of two and a half years' imprisonment as a result. In prison, he organized a circle for Marxist studies and learned some technology; when he came out, he had advanced TB.

He was arrested for the third time when he was a storekeeper. A large State Agricultural Co-operative had no weighbridge. The weight of the transports of fodder had to be assessed by sight. When the state-owned horses and cattle began to die from chronic undernourishment, Konieczny was arrested. He was released a month later, declared innocent, but in prison he had developed a mild form of persecution mania which was to lead him eventually to the psychiatric clinic where he would write his appeal to the First Secretary of the Party.

Solshenitsin's big novel about Stalin's Russia is located in a cancer ward. Cancer attacks indiscriminately party and non-party people, officers of the NKVD and prisoners of camps, executioners and their victims. For Solshenitsin the cancer hospital was the only place in the USSR where no one was afraid to speak the truth. Andrzejewski has located his *Appeal* in a psychiatric clinic. But in order to see the truth, one must first of all emerge from insanity. Marian Konieczny, that rag of a man, with his life ruined by cruel times and an even more cruel system, sees around him only imaginary persecutors: thousands of agents of the ' Counter-intelligence ' sent out by an electronic brain who watch him, ape all his gestures and don't give him a moment's peace. But even to that ruin of a man comes a short flash of revelation, when he is able to see human and divine injustice: '. . . what, I ask, can the people and the nation do if there are no just men at the top, if it is the devils who hold the power and say to the nation: " We shall make angels of you ", yet behave in such a way and oppress people so that a devil's own brew comes of it? Where is there any help or salvation? It is idle to call for help, no one will hear and even if they did, they wouldn't understand . . .'

In 1947, at about the same time that the security officer held his conversation with Konieczny, I went to Moscow with a delegation of Polish writers for the annual celebration of the November Revolution. Boris Pasternak was not included among the writers who had welcomed us. He was in disgrace and not allowed to meet foreign guests, not even the writers from a ' brotherly Socialist country '. Through mutual friends, he sent me a message that he would expect me at his country house near Moscow. I was advised to tell our official guardians that I felt unwell and could not attend supper, but would rest in my hotel room. Late in the evening someone came to fetch me; we changed cars twice and around midnight I found myself in Pasternak's house. I stayed with him until daybreak. I spoke to Pasternak about the revolution which had taken place in Poland and the free discussions being held about the future of Socialist literature. Pasternak remained silent for a long time and kept smiling. 'You are like little birds,' he said at last, 'chirrupping in the forest. Each of you still chirrups in his own voice. But soon a day will dawn when you will wake up and see that each of you is in a separate cage. Under one of the cages there will be a sign: "Ex-Formalist", under another: "Ex-Symbolist", under yet another: "Ex-Surrealist". You will all be classified. And over all the cages, there will be a large panel with the words: "Enemies of the People ".'

When I returned to Warsaw, on the building where the Writers' Union was housed, a large red sheet was hanging with the inscription: 'Writers – the engineers of human souls!' Inside the Union's premises there was an announcement on the board about the opening of training courses in Marxism. Only a few Polish writers realized at the time that their cages were being prepared. We found ourselves inside them very soon afterwards. But nearly ten years were to pass before I myself and my closest literary friends noticed that we were inside cages which we ourselves had helped to build.

In 1957, Andrzejewski published a novel entitled *Darkness Obscures the Earth* (English title: *The Inquisitors*). He was one of the first Polish writers who were Party members to emerge from darkness. When the Polish 'October' proved to be nothing more than a nine-days' wonder and 'Socialism with a human face' one more bitter illusion, Andrzejewski left the Party. In 1968, he was one of the few writers in Poland publicly to dare protest against the invasion of Czechoslovakia. *The Inquisitors* was a novel about a Great Inquisitor and his fanatical disciple to whom the Master revealed before his death his doubts about the infallibility of the doctrine. The disciple desecrated the Master's body after his death. *The Gates of Paradise*, the next of Andrzejewski's novels, is a shattering tale about the medieval crusade of fanatical children to the Holy Land. But as soon as Andrzejewski cast off the parables and removed the historical costumes of his heroes, his subsequent books did not get published in Poland. Like Solshenitsin in Russia, he is his country's Great Dumb Man.

In 1954, I went with a delegation of Polish writers to China for a change. Our hosts allowed us very unwillingly to walk in the streets. But one evening at Shanghai they took us to a public park. Two children came up to us, a girl of about five and a boy of about seven years of age. They were both in rags and begged for something to eat. I began to say to our guides that five years is not enough to get the better of hunger . . . They interrupted me, looked sternly at me and said: 'Look, Comrade, at these begging children; there are no such children in China.'

Jan Kott

THE Clinic for Psychosomatic Diseases, Block Number 9, stands densely surrounded by trees in the spacious grounds of the City Hospital at T. This quiet, picturesque city on the Vistula, rich in historical monuments, is not now the administrative centre of a province nor does it boast any important industries; it enjoys none the less, all over the country, the fame of an old and distinguished university centre. Block 9, along with most of the hospital buildings, dates from the first half of the nineteenth century, but the mellowness of its walls speaks of neglect rather than historical importance. Its interior, damaged during the war and since redecorated only once, in 1946, when it was also re-equipped by UNRRA, is cramped, its ground plan anachronistically faithful to the requirements of medical science of many years ago. In spite of its shortcomings, however, it has become a centre where the most complex problems of confused and suffering human minds can be solved thanks to the devoted enthusiasm and steadfast energy of Registrar Dr Stefan Plebanski, the director of the Clinic, and the team of young doctors of both sexes whom he has carefully selected.

Dr Plebanski, a middle-aged psychiatrist, had to overcome numerous obstacles, prejudices and even superstitions at various levels in the bureaucratic hierarchy before he was able to organize the psychosomatic unit at the City Hospital at T in the early sixties and to obtain for it from the outset the status of a University Clinic. Insisting stubbornly, sometimes against the interests of his own career, that a unit of that kind should be formed, he was motivated by the simple belief that not all mentally sick people required treatment in specialized hospitals, which cater in the first place for chronic or incurable diseases and are moreover – like the institutions at Tworki, Drewnica or Kobierzyn – associated in the public mind with the evil stigma of life-long mania and madness. Even people who are pronounced cured return to life from these institutions with a feeling of shame, as if they had been branded. The Clinic for Psychosomatic Diseases, forgoing the debased term 'psychiatric' even in its official title, was to occupy, according to Dr Plebanski's intentions, a position intermediate between a psychiatric institution and an ordinary hospital. In practice this position gave rise to rather peculiar conditions inside the clinic: thus a thorough search of personal belongings, well secured windows, the absence of knives at mealtimes, wards with compulsorily open doors and a number of minor rules co-existed with passes being granted to some patients to leave the clinic on Saturdays or even for whole week-ends. The so-called 'psychologist's room' constituted a similar concession.

The constant proximity of the patients to one another in the clinic sometimes helped towards the social re-education of individuals whose family and occupational ties, instead of remaining a sturdy cord accepted voluntarily and eagerly, had become dangerously frayed to a fine thread. But there are times when a patient, in order to regain a precarious equilibrium, needs a few hours of solitude which is only seemingly anti-social, because the concentrated facing of his own self helps him to strengthen that frail thread in harmony with his own nature. For the benefit of such individuals, Dr Plebanski, having overcome many economic and administrative obstacles, had managed to discover on the second floor of the block housing the clinic a modest little room which, after an inexpensive face-lift, was transformed from an attic junk-room into a quiet little study, with a desk, a couple of armchairs, a sofa and a direct telephone line to town. Thanks to this modest investment, an eminent psychologist of the University of T could three times a week give the patients consultations beneficial to their state of mind. Hence the name of the little study, which also, with Dr Plebanski's special permission, could be used in the afternoons by some patients for a few hours' solitude which might help their recovery. Naturally, it was mostly the intellectuals and artists who used the ' psychologist's room '; those who, as a result of painful embroilments with life and their own personalities, sought with Dr Plebanski's medical – and for the uninitiated somewhat magical – help a refuge at the clinic and a strengthening of their weakened relationships.

It was therefore a highly untypical event when, some time in October 1967, one of the patients, a certain Marian Konieczny, aged 41, domiciled at O, married, by occupation a technologist in the meat-products industry but already pensioned off, personally applied to the Registrar for permission to use the psychologist's room for a few afternoons.

Permission was granted straightaway and he was not even asked for what purpose he required solitude and quiet. This discretion on the Registrar's part – a proof of his confidence in the non-typical patient – deeply moved Konieczny; and the equilibrium already achieved after more than a month's stay in the clinic prevented him from reacting with the helpless childlike sobbing of which he had experienced three prolonged attacks in the last four years, and which had compelled him to seek Dr Plebanski's help. So Konieczny did not burst into tears, but, confronted with such touching generosity on the Doctor's part, felt obliged to reciprocate with a similar proof of loyalty. He was moved to say to the Registrar:

' I must explain to you, Mr Registrar, why I need a little calm. You have always been like a father to me, so I have no secrets from you, as if you were my real father, and don't wish to have any, you will always give me good advice, I know. So this is how it is, Mr Registrar, I have thought about it in detail, I have been thinking and thinking about it for days on end, and at night when I wake up and cannot sleep. I think about it all the time. No, Mr Registrar, please don't be afraid, I am not getting excited, I am calm and thinking calmly, it's my leg that gets excited but I know it will pass when I go back home and start living normally with my wife, otherwise I am completely calm and therefore, having thought about my case in detail, I have come to the conclusion that my only salvation is to seek human justice, for I don't fear God's justice, the Lord won't refuse to let me go to Heaven after the hell I've been through on earth. Therefore in connection with my case, Mr Registrar, I know your opinion in this respect, but I swear on all that is holy, on the happiness of my children, on everything that is dear to me, on the heads of my sons so that they may be spared such sufferings as I their father have been subjected to, this is not my delusion, I can discriminate. I also have irrefutable proof, I might sometimes be wrong, but my basic discrimination is correct, so that after careful thinking I have come to the conclusion that I must now do everything to prove my innocence so that after twelve years they should stop their devilish tricks with me and justice can be done, for the wrong that has been done to me is not my own personal wrong. I, Mr Registrar, have always been a socially conscious individual, therefore if I have suffered such grievous and unjust wrongs the whole community is affected by it. Am I not right, Mr Registrar?'

' So what have you decided, Mr Konieczny?' asked Dr Plebanski.

' I have decided to appeal to the very top. Those at the top should be informed about my wrong, they should consider everything in their conscience as citizens and weigh it up, and then give a just verdict, because I believe, Mr Registrar, and this is my conviction, that at the top they know nothing about my misfortune, those devils from the Counter-intelligence must certainly hide their tricks from them, but I trust, Mr Registrar, that as soon as they learn at the top, then an order will come that I am innocent and pure as the driven snow and none of my bitter enemies will dare torture me, justice will be done, the slanderous persecutions will cease, truth will triumph and I shall be publicly rehabilitated so that I can walk about with my head held high and not be afraid to look people in the eye. Am I not right, Mr Registrar?'

In a few careful words Konieczny was reassured on that score. Thus spiritually comforted, he continued:

'Had I not been socially conscious, Mr Registrar, I would have recommended myself to God's mercy and would have disregarded all those plots and said: go on, go on, you mad devils, search if you like, but you'll find nothing, for, so help me God, I have never been a traitor to my country, have never served any foreign intelligence service, have always served the Motherland and the People's Government, have never spared my health, working as much as my strength and skill allowed. But because I am socially conscious I want to find justice here on this earth, therefore I have decided to describe all my life in detail, concealing nothing, writing only the truth and sending this letter, when I have finished, to the highest authorities in the People's Government. Let them learn what has been done to a loyal son of the nation. I don't fear their verdict, I know that my sufferings will be justly weighed and judged by the Citizen First Secretary. For these above-stated reasons I have permitted myself to ask you, Mr Registrar, to allow me to use the psychologist's room. I shall describe everything I have told you in detail, and when I have finished, before sending it off to the Citizen First Secretary, I shall give it to you to read, Mr Registrar, and shall be obliged for any corrections, my spelling might not be all it should be, I did not have the benefits of full education, not like the young people now . . .'

Thus on the very same day – it was a Monday and the weather was very beautiful, warm and sunny – promptly at three o'clock in the afternoon, when many of the patients, individually or under the supervision of a member of the staff, were going downstairs for a walk in the hospital garden, Konieczny, having previously obtained from the doctor on duty the key to the psychologist's room and reported where necessary before doing so, made his way to the second floor, equipped with his working tools, namely an ordinary school exercise book and a cheap ball-point pen, both objects purchased at the local newspaper kiosk during his morning walk.

Konieczny's first action when he found himself in the psychologist's room was to turn the key in the door. At once, however, he realized that if any of the doctors came on an inspection and found the door locked from the inside, he might misinterpret things to the detriment of the person inside. He therefore unlocked the door again, and then stood still for a moment listening to see if anybody was walking up the stairs. Nobody was, there was silence, an unbelievable silence. He found himself within it as under a glass bell fitted with precision to the shape of the room, so that he stood there sunk in the silence and stunned, almost unnerved by its immobility; he instinctively tried to hold his breath, or to breathe as lightly as he could to ascertain if the silence would deepen and he breathed out with relief when, from the floor below, he heard a door bang and from the characteristic noise that followed he realized that a new group of patients was going out for a walk. Only then, as if that slight commotion downstairs had given him support, did he tiptoe to the desk and lay upon it the exercise book and ball-point pen. He intended to move the chair so that, without wasting time, he might start his urgent work, but his eyes, not yet familiarized with his surroundings, glided from the desk top to the wooden floor recently washed – its rough surface was still damp here and there – then wandered higher and rested on the autumnal but still lush greenness of an enormous chestnut tree; in the dense expanse of thick branches and leaves his eyes detected a rust-coloured patch, immobile but with shiny eyes. Instinctively, not knowing why he did it, he lifted his hand and then, although he was not very near and although they were separated by the window pane, the rusty patch became a living flame, almost licking the window before disappearing at once somewhere higher up; only the leaves, no more than an arm's length away, swayed for a while. 'Just think, just think!' Konieczny whispered softly and felt that a good cry would relieve his feelings. But he did not cry; he walked over to the window and, resting his hands on the sill and his forehead against the cool pane, began to look for the squirrel in the top branches of the chestnut tree, above which spread the smooth and clear blue of the sky; he did not see the squirrel, although he stood for a long while with his head upturned. At last he returned to the desk, sat down, opened the exercise book and on the first page wrote in a large and round hand the address, name, Christian name and Party position of the addressee, and added a moment later: Central Committee of the Polish United Workers' Party, Warsaw. Then he laid down the pen and felt tired and sleepy, so he propped his head on his hand and in that position of concentrated musing Konieczny was found at half past five by the short, dark-haired pretty Sister Irene who came upstairs to remind him that it was time to come down to supper.

The next day was cloudy, with a thin rain falling, and it looked like autumn out of doors. After the morning doctors' rounds Konieczny played bridge, lost two rubbers with

THE APPEAL

eleven points and won one, finishing with a small slam in diamonds and ended three points up.

In spite of this satisfaction he began to complain of great restlessness, and although his partners had asked him to play another rubber he stopped and retired to his room. He lay on his bed in his usual daily position – on his back, both hands under his head, his right leg, which suffered from a nervous tic (a side-effect of tranquillizers) loosely dangling in a position that allowed him to sway it freely. After dinner (prune soup with noodles and boiled beef with potatoes and shredded beetroot) he lay down again, swung his leg for another fifteen minutes at least, after which he fell asleep, still on his back, and began to snore heavily, much to the displeasure of one of his room-mates, a young Frenchman, Jean-Claude Caron, a lecturer at the University of T. Caron, who dabbled in journalism and translations and who had only recently appeared in the clinic, was dark and slim, very Western European, but at the same time very restless and unnaturally over-excited. He had become addicted lately to sleeping pills; he would swallow five or six of them regularly at seven pm and at eight pm, fall heavily asleep, only to wake up at four in the morning in a state of euphoria and artificially stimulated energy which somewhat compensated for the innaccessibility of great boulevards, bistros and *frutti di mare*. He would then work until the following evening, keeping himself going by cups of extra-strong instant coffee, red wine and strong spirits. Now, deprived of all that stimulated his creativity, he was missing the pleasures of over-excitement and slowly, although not without abortive attempts at revolt, sinking into a slough of sweaty depression. Konieczny's snoring, by

9

day and by night, released in Caron the remains of his diminishing energy. Incapable for the moment of working, or even reading properly, he limited himself to a tortured peering at the front page of one issue of *Le Monde,* not touching the issues that followed. Yet Konieczny's snoring aggravated Caron to such an extent that whenever he heard it he turned heavily on his bed, making the springs vibrate violently, sighed loudly and with a noisy determination cleared his throat and coughed. But all his efforts were in vain; Konieczny, once he had fallen asleep, could sleep undisturbed even if the earth were to shake and thunderbolts fall around him. On the other hand, another two of Konieczny's companions in room No 30 did not react at all to his snoring, and slept like stones rolled down a deep well: they were a certain Colonel of the Frontier Corps, suffering from chronic depression, and a sixteen-year-old called Raphael, just undergoing insulin shock treatment for the suspected onset of juvenile schizophrenia.

Thus the morning and early afternoon of that Tuesday passed uneventfully for Konieczny. He woke up at a quarter to three and less than twenty minutes later, having obtained the key from Dr Konarska, the lady doctor on duty, he went upstairs to the psychologist's room. There he switched on the ceiling light because, despite the still early hour of the day, the room was in semi-darkness. He looked for a moment from the window at the chestnut tree. Since the day before it seemed to have shed some of its leaves, and the remaining ones, appearing more yellow, were now being buffeted by a strong wind. He drew the curtains together, switched on the desk lamp, took the exercise book and pen out of the pocket of his hospital robe, and set to work.

THE APPEAL

During that afternoon he wrote the following:

I the undersigned Marian Konieczny, son of John and Aniela (née Kundicz) Konieczny, born on 1st May 1926 in the village of Kalety, district of Augustow, by occupation technologist in the meat-products industry, pensioned off in 1964, domiciled at O – 17 Victory Avenue, flat number 5B – at present undergoing treatment at the Psychosomatic Clinic of the City Hospital at T under the care of Citizen Registrar Dr Stefan Plebanski – have the honour to apply to you, Citizen First Secretary, with the earnest request that you consider my letter personally, in view of the fact that I have been terribly and innocently wronged and, although for the last twelve years I have been persecuted by members of the Counter-intelligence and have suffered a great deal, have been unable to find justice anywhere – therefore I am appealing to you, Citizen First Secretary, because I believe that you, Citizen First Secretary, will deal with my case like a father and pass a just verdict, and also give instructions that my merciless persecutors should cease their machinations for although I am not and never have been a Party member, I have always loyally served People's Poland, have never been anybody's agent or a traitor, and if I have committed mistakes, it was from ignorance, because I did not complete my schooling, although I wanted to do so very much indeed and have tried all my life to improve my education. I ask you not to be angry, Citizen First Secretary, if you find faults in my style, but instead I shall try to write from the heart and tell you the whole truth, and I also ask you most earnestly, Citizen First Secretary, for the great favour to pass a just verdict after getting acquainted with the present material, because I am suffering a great deal innocently and have no strength to suffer any longer. Now I am fit again thanks to the efforts and care of Citizen Registrar Dr Plebanski, but before arriving here, I never stopped crying and things were bad with me and when they are bad, Citizen First Secretary, they are quite terrible, so terrible and gruesome that I cannot express it, I feel that inside me there is too much of something, but I can't say what and this is what is so terrible and frightening, sometimes it seems to me that I have a cold cellar inside me, another time – a red-hot cauldron, and then I think that I will catch fire and live flames will blaze in me, and my bones begin to weaken as if they were made of wax, may God forgive my persecutors for my terrible misfortune, because I cannot forgive them. I forgot to mention, Citizen First Secretary, that when I have a cellar inside me, my bones feel differently, they too begin to freeze and stiffen, this is really horrible and frightening and I have to take a firm hold on myself not to go mad, but such an effort is very weakening, and when I have made it I feel exhausted and therefore afterwards I get easily moved and begin to cry, but after each weeping I feel even weaker. Often I cannot stand upright because my legs give way and my hands tremble, so I must sit down and cannot do anything, not even household chores, for since the time I was pensioned off, i.e. 1st January 1964, all the household duties have rested on me, my wife Halina Konieczna (née Tomaszewska) works on the railway, in the Department of Statistics and Planning of the Polish State Railways, Region Gdansk, and we have three sons, Alexander, born in 1954, John, born in 1955, and Michael, born in 1957, our housing conditions are

below the norm, for a co-operative flat has been allotted us
for 1969, we are still waiting for my wife to be given a sub-
stitute flat until 1969, but my persecutors secretly and
stealthily spoil my chances of bettering my daily life, so we
live with my wife and sons in the flat of my brother-in-law,
Citizen Victor Tomaszewski, my wife's brother, it is a very
small flat, two rooms and a kitchen, thirty-four square
metres in all, on the fifth floor, so there is often no water
because of insufficient pressure, sometimes the taps are
empty all day and one can only get water late in the evening or more often in the middle of the night.

My brother-in-law, Victor Tomaszewski, has three children as well, a boy and two girls, and because of his chronic
lumbago he has also been pensioned off, by trade he is a
mycologist, so he is not doing too badly as a pensioner because he gets commissions, but my wife and I don't need
anything from him, we pay our share of the rent and all
other expenses regularly, because we try to manage so that
our budget is stabilized but it is very hard to share a flat
even with one's nearest family, a cultivated person suffers
from sharing a kitchen, and my brother-in-law is rather vio-
lent by nature, he likes a drink too, and when he has had too
much he gets pains and becomes touchy and offensive,
makes a scene about nothing, and our wives, that is to say
my wife and his, Ursula, are nervy too, and haven't got
much sympathy for one another, the children are the ones
who suffer most from these scenes. I am the only one who
tries to smooth down these above-mentioned controversies,
and this makes my nerves become frayed: a man could
endure worse things, quarrels occur in the best families,
the worst thing is that my persecutors have penetrated

insidiously into my closest circle, into my nearest family and
so skilfully have they insinuated themselves by perfidious
machinations that – I won't say my wife, for I cannot say
anything against her, she is kind to me and the children, a
little untidy perhaps and too fond of male company, but not
too much, so I don't accuse my wife of anything – but my
brother-in-law and perhaps sister-in-law too have been in-
fluenced by them. At first I didn't suspect anything, but
later those people from the Counter-intelligence began to
act more and more boldly, watching my every step so that
they could ape me, Citizen First Secretary. One day in
1964 I slept a little longer than usual in the morning and
was alone in our room, because my wife had gone to work
and my sons to school, so before breakfast, to freshen myself up, I sprayed my hair with a hairdressing lotion made
by Viola at Gliwice and combed it in front of a mirror, and
then went into the kitchen to heat up some milk, and suddenly, while I was walking along the passage, I saw the door
to my brother-in-law's room half-open, and usually he kept
it shut, and when I looked that way a shiver ran down my
spine, I stopped breathing and began to tremble so much
that I had to support myself against the chest of drawers
standing in the passage so as not to fall. And the thing that
shocked me so, Citizen First Secretary, was that my brother-
in-law was spraying his hair with a lotion and combing it in
front of a mirror, just like I had done, I don't even know,
Citizen First Secretary, who I felt sorry for first: myself –
because the enemy had penetrated into my room, shamelessly using a member of my family, or him – that he let
himself be bribed, like Judas, and if not bribed, which I
can't quite believe, then that he was mean enough to

believe the hostile whispers that I, his own brother-in-law, have become the agent of an enemy intelligence service. I remember that when the first weakness passed and I could move my legs again, I thought: Oh, no, brother, I won't let this pass so easily, you must know that I'm not blind or deaf and have a clear understanding of what is being cooked up around me and what a bad joke citizen brother-in-law has agreed to play on me, so I entered the room, I can't remember whether I said good morning or not, but I remember that when he saw me come in, he looked at me askance like people do who have a bad conscience, but he did not interrupt that Judas combing of his hair, he continued to work on it, only he was nervous now, the comb was moving in his hand as fast as if it was being run by electric current, and with his other hand he manipulated the mirror – it was the same kind of mirror as mine – he moved it first to one side of his head, then to the other side, and I must explain here that my brother-in-law has a miserable hair growth, he is getting as bald as a jacket worn at the elbows, so that the comb was of little use on his miserable few hairs, also I had never before seen him devote so much effort and care to his appearance, but I was not really astonished, for I realized at once where the essence of the problem lies and that he, the treacherous Judas of a brother-in-law, did not attach any importance to the care of his hair, but had been ordered from above, or given a sly hint to give me a sign that THEY are keeping an eye on me and watching and taking note of every one of my activities even at home.

Well then, as he had already moved to the enemy camp, when I entered the room – which I didn't do very often – and I can't remember whether I said good morning or not,

he looked at me askance and went on manipulating his comb
and mirror, and I asked calmly, not letting on: 'Doing
your hair?' and he, not yet an ace in the art of spying, got
terribly embarrassed, so that his neck became quite red –
my brother-in-law is getting fat, his paunch is growing fast
– but he must have twigged, for he puffed out his cheeks, as
he often does, pushed his stomach out and mumbled something into the mirror like: 'What of it?' at least I thought
it was 'What of it?' to which I said never averting my eyes
from him: 'And you have sprinkled your hair with lotion?'
then he said: 'Don't you like it?' and I said: 'Oh yes,
quite, why shouldn't I like it? I even like your comb and
mirror.' I waited to see what he would say, well, then he
said it, putting the mirror on the table and pulling up his
trousers, for they were slipping down over his paunch:
'Listen, Marian,' he said, 'you mind your own business,
that's my advice.' 'I know,' I answered, 'that's good advice,
I know it very well.' Then he said, and his neck became red
again: 'If you know it, then get off my back and shut the
door after you.' Quite in order, I thought to myself – to pre-
tend, little brother, you haven't learnt yet – and I wanted
to leave the room, when suddenly what do I see? On the
back of a chair, next to the unmade bed, a new jacket was
hanging, I could swear it was new, I had never seen him in
one like this, a grey jacket with a darker herringbone
pattern, and his nylon shirt also seemed new and of foreign
origin, my Judas of a brother-in-law must have bought the
clobber in the commission shop in May-the-First Street, a
side street from Freedom Square. The next day I checked
on everything and I was right, I quite often get a sudden intuition like that and can assess facts correctly and

accurately, so that when I saw my house spy's clobber thrown on the chair anyhow, I at once remembered that my brother-in-law had returned home late, after ten, and it was easy to guess that he was quite merry, because he didn't pay any attention to the fact that my wife and I had put the light out, he has never been attentive at the best of times, but when he has been drinking he behaves like a person without any breeding at all – everything became clear to me, a person can lie, but facts never lie, you must just arrange them properly, so although my hands had begun to tremble and I could hardly breathe, I tried not to show anything and asked: 'How much did they give you?' And then he put his comb on the table next to the mirror and asked in a hoarse voice: 'I don't understand what you mean?' 'You do, you do,' I said, and had to lean against the table for my hands began to shake again. 'You know very well what I mean.' 'Perhaps you do,' said my new persecutor, 'but I don't.' He was defending himself stupidly, you could see he was new to the spy game, so I decided to come into the open and looked him straight in the eye and said: 'How many Judas pieces did they give you to recruit you? A thousand, two thousand or perhaps five? Tell me, don't be ashamed to admit how many Judas pieces you're earning on your own brother-in-law?' Then I thought he would have a stroke but no, he was tough and apparently ready for anything, for he only puffed heavily as if he wanted to unplug the words which stuck in his throat, then he banged his fist on the table and screamed: 'Push off, will you, at once! Play your silly tricks on lunatics like you are yourself, but not on me!' Very well, I thought, he has weak nerves, it's clear he could not stand it and has unmasked himself, so I have nothing more to do for I have learned everything. I left the room and shut the door after me and then, while standing in the dark passage, something strange happened to me, so that I forgot for a moment where I was and didn't know whether it was day or night. I only felt quite frozen inside and my hands kept shaking: I don't know how long this condition lasted, but I remember that the first thing I noticed was daylight from the end of the passage, so I went towards it and found myself in the kitchen, and when I got there I remembered everything that had happened and felt so weak that I had to sit down on the nearest stool, and when I sat down I was filled with such sadness and sorrow that I began to cry and I must have cried for a long time, for I heard someone enter the kitchen, stop in the doorway, and then come up to me and put his hand on my shoulder. I wanted to stop crying but I couldn't, because the weeping grew in me until I heard next to me my Judas-brother-in-law's voice, gentle and soft. 'Marian,' he said, 'calm down for goodness' sake. I got angry unnecessarily, it's my fault, I apologize, Marian.' And while he was saying it I went on weeping, although I didn't want to, and while I was weeping I kept thinking how oddly this world of ours has been arranged, for not only the downtrodden and persecuted people suffer in it, but also the others; the persecutors and oppressors, O Lord Almighty, Jesus Christ Our Most Merciful Lord, I should like to know whether those who force people to persecute others also suffer when they are alone, Jesus Christ Our Lord . . .

*

THE APPEAL

On Wednesday, the third day of work on his petition to the highest authorities, Konieczny continued:

Yesterday I rather diverged from my plan, for a painful and unpleasant memory got hold of me, and so now, to present and explain my case fully, I shall describe my life in the sequence in which it has brought me various sorrows and worries as well as a few rays of joy and some successes in my work, from the day of my birth until the day of my great misfortune, I shall describe the events of my life in the same order in which I related them orally at the suggestion of Registrar Dr Plebanski and in his presence during my first stay in the clinic in July 1963. That first stay and treatment lasted exactly two months and I left the clinic calm and fit, but my enemies were quick to remember me and got on to me again, so that the campaign against me continued and I experienced various intrigues and general discrimination against me in my work so my nerves failed me again, and to escape from my persecutors I had to hide with Registrar Dr Plebanski, who has always been friendly and kind to me, which is an honour and a great consolation for me. This was in January 1964, when I again spent two months in the clinic, and my enemies, in spite of using the Electronic Brain and an enormous number of agents and spies, lost track of me in the end and didn't know where I was, and this is why my hiding-place in the clinic is a great support and help to me, I don't know what I would do if I lost this safe place, because here I am calm and without fear.

I was born on 1st May 1926 in the village of Kalety, district of Augustow, of Jan Konieczny and Aniela (née

Kundicz), of landowning origin. My grandfather, Alexander
Kundicz, lost his lands after the Rising of 1863 and as a
youth in his twenties was exiled to Siberia where his fiancée,
Barbara Owerllo, loyally followed him, there my maternal
grandparents got married and afterwards lived in want for
long years in the Department of Tambov and when my
grandfather died his widow, Barbara Kundicz, with her son
Olgierd (who later became a Communist and disappeared
without trace in 1936) and daughter Aniela returned to her
native district, supporting herself as a tailoress, and it was at
Augustow that my father met my mother, they were drawn
to each other by a great romantic love which led them to the
altar, although my father was a simple peasant and a
forester, and my mother poor and uneducated but all the
same a member of the old and once rich family of Kundicz
(Korab coat of arms). Until People's Poland broke out, distant relatives of my mother, also Kundiczes, had landed
estates in the region of Sandomierz, but my mother had
never been in contact with them. My father had a very hard
and poverty-stricken childhood, didn't finish at any school,
but learnt forestry practically, and was later employed in the
forests of Ciercierz, and this is why I spent my childhood
in forests. Before the outbreak of the war I managed to get
through six forms of primary school at the village of Ciercierz and planned at the time to follow in my father's foot-
steps and become a forester, because I loved nature and this
work seemed suited to my disposition. The war, however,
let loose by Nazi imperialism, upset all my beautiful plans,
although for the first four years I escaped by being under
age; I had a lot of free time, so I helped my father, but
mostly helped in the household because my father's second

wife, Bronislawa Konieczna (née Kowalczyk), began to sicken in the winter of 1941 and became so weak that she couldn't undertake any of the harder domestic tasks, and died after great suffering on 23rd November 1943 in the hospital at Augustow of cancer of the stomach, so that there was no hope for her. She was a good stepmother, always caring for us, that is for my brothers and sisters and myself, as if we were her own children, and there were six of us in all – the oldest, Alexander, born in 1914, Barbara born in 1918, Aniela born in 1920, Yadwiga born in 1922 and Stanislaw born in 1924. I had two more brothers, of whom one, Zbigniew, born in 1916, died of diphtheria in early childhood, and the last of all, Witold, born in 1929, lived for only a few hours and his coming caused the premature death of my mother. I can't remember my mother at all, for when she died in childbirth on 11th October 1929 I was three years old, from photographs I remember that she was a comely woman, my father as a young man was also goodlooking, tall and strongly built, my brother Alexander took after him, perhaps also Stanislaw, I don't look like my father, I am one metre sixty-seven centimetres tall, proportionately built and fairly strong, and my light brown hair used to be thick and grow on my head like a helmet, only in the last few years as a result of my horrible tragedy it has begun to thin out and I have also put on weight, because I don't get enough exercise.

After the unexpected death of my mother, my father found himself in mourning and in a difficult situation, for what was he to do with such a bunch of small children who needed a woman's care? Father was not doing too badly, but mainly because my mother was a loyal wife and a good manager, so after his mourning was over, father again got married. He met my future stepmother at the hospital at Augustow where my mother had her last confinement and died, my stepmother was working there as a non-qualified nurse and therefore, as far back as I can remember, she has always been very clean and paid much attention to hygiene, which was very rare in the country in those days. I remember she always made us wash our hands before sitting down to a meal, there were many difficulties in this respect with my brother Stanislaw – I also clearly remember that my stepmother always made sure that the toilet was clean, and this was long before the Prime Minister of that time, General Slavoy-Skladkowski, began personal visits to the countryside inspecting in particular the little outhouses in the villages and ordering them to be whitewashed and this is why these outhouses were often called ' Slavoys ' after his name. I used to be able to remember a lot of things from my childhood, but now, although I am only just over forty, my memory has been considerably weakened, and this is because of my persecutors of the Counter-intelligence and that's what I cannot forgive them, because a person's childhood and his family and home should be precious to him, unless they were very sad and unhappy, but my childhood was not unhappy, although we did not have much comfort or any money to spare, therefore I cannot forgive my oppressors that they have stolen my childhood from me and now, when I am sad and depressed, I don't find solace in harking back to those distant days: immediately after the war I could still remember a lot from my childhood, and in prison, I recall, I could console myself with shining memories and they were like a magic elixir of life for me, in my compulsory detention, but now since the time when, quite innocent, I fell foul of party bosses who don't abide by the law themselves, I have been so worn down by intrigues and incessant persecution that I have lost my childhood, probably for ever. I often sit and think and think, and I try to remind myself of the land of childish games, but I cannot remember anything, not even when I see forests around me in my mind, I never know whether these are the forests of my first childish steps and boyish pranks, or other forests which I got to know afterwards – my father appears to me as he was in his old age, and I see my brothers and sisters as grown-up people too, I am heartbroken that the memories of my childhood are so poor – one memory that has remained is when my eldest brother, Alexander, came home for his holidays from Augustow where he was going to college and got an air-gun from my father, I don't know precisely how old I was, but I must have been very small, perhaps three or four years old, and one day my brother was trying to shoot a squirrel, I can hear the report of the gun even now and when I close my eyes I can see the small red creature, which a moment before had been jumping gracefully from branch to branch and enjoying life, fall like a stone from the tall tree: when it lay on the ground I rushed up to it, its paws were curled up and its eyes closed, it seemed asleep, only from its mouth ran a rivulet of blood: when I went to the country, to Cierlica, for my father's funeral, in March 1959, I met my sister Yadwiga, who had come with her two children from as far away as Walbrzych, where her husband, Andrew Kobiela, is an engineer in the Boleslaw Bierut mine, then she told me, when we spoke about old times, that after the shooting of that squirrel I couldn't sleep all night and had a high temperature, but even she couldn't remember how old I was, probably four, so this must have happened thirty-seven years ago, a whole life-span ago – my wretched life is as good as finished, although I don't give up hope that you, Citizen First Secretary . . .

I feel very tired and have no strength to go on writing, I have cramp in my hand and my head is beginning to ache and I feel restless, but I have so much work to do tomorrow, the day after tomorrow and so on – I am panic-stricken how I shall cope, and yet my only hope is this letter. I wonder what my wife is doing now, she must have returned home from the office, perhaps not yet, for she has to do her shopping on the way home and at this time the queues are longest, poor woman, not only has she got to work hard but when I am away all the housekeeping is her responsibility, and the children as well, we have three boys, Alexander born in 1954, John born in 1955 and Michael born in 1957, thank goodness they are all healthy and surprisingly good-looking, I cannot think how, for Halina is no Miss Beauty, although she has a pleasant appearance, and I am no Adonis, although in my youth I was not at all bad-looking, yet we have handsome children, everybody says so, and quite bright, but they don't care much about school and have to be watched to do their homework properly, Alec is only thirteen but soon he will be as tall as I am or taller, he already reaches my shoulder, I have been planning for a long time for him to study law after secondary school, so that he can defend those who are unjustly accused, or sit at a judge's bench, to punish criminals on behalf of People's Poland and discharge those who are innocent, for the moment Alec is a fine and bright boy, but he is only interested in sport and can remember all our own records and world records better than the things he is being taught at school, and this is why he had to repeat the fifth class, I am worried about his progress now that I am away, but console myself that when he grows up he will be more sensible and will understand that at present a man without education is like a cripple, although it is also true to say that a miner, a steel worker, a qualified lathe operator or a welder earns more in a month than for instance a doctor of medicine, but higher education is higher education.

I must be content with what I have achieved by hard work, but it is my duty to help the children to grow up into cultured people and if Alec does not want to study law, I shall try to push Johnny in that direction, for the youngest, Mickey, shows quite different talents, he is ten now, but moves gracefully and prettily, he's lively like a spark, always smiling and wants to dance all the time, my wife says that we must definitely send him to a ballet school, perhaps she is right, she has a good instinct for these things, mothers are seldom wrong about their children, only it seems strange to me that my son should become a dancer and perform publicly on the stage, be given applause and become famous perhaps, I should like to see it, it must be a great happiness to be able to dance for the pleasure of other people and make them forget their worries and hardships for at least a few hours, I should like my little Mickey to bring such magic to people, I won't be here to see it, but Halina perhaps, she deserves it for all the . . .

Thursday

I am very restless today, because yesterday evening at nine o'clock a terrible accident happened, a patient who arrived a few days ago from Warsaw committed suicide, a doctor of medicine, named Kalinski or Kalecki, I didn't hear exactly what his name was, he was having a bath and the ward nurse Wirtek looked in a few times to see how he was getting on, and then went for a moment to the male section of the clinic, because Grandpa had again wetted his bed and when Wirtek was seeing to him the ward nurse began to scream, I was watching television, which because of lack of space is placed in the corridor of the women's section, they were showing a film about the great Polish scientist, Maria Curie-Sklodowska, it was then that the doctor cut his throat with a razor blade, no one knows where he got it from, because he used to shave with an electric razor, he must have pinched it from somewhere or concealed it, Sister Irena whom I like a lot said he was already dead when they found him in the bath, being a doctor he knew precisely how to kill himself, I saw him being carried out of the bathroom covered in blood, but I didn't see his head because I turned back so as not to see, and then Wirtek locked the door. I went to bed when they carried him out, everybody was very agitated, but I was most angry that the Frenchman, when he turned in, ate some cheese and then an apple, we all switched off the light, only he didn't, I was terribly angry that he was eating that apple and, as he has good teeth, each time he took a bite there was a loud crunch, I couldn't stand it and said: 'Jesus Christ, Mr Caron, when will you stop eating that apple?' I thought he would be cross, because he has a southern temperament, but he was not cross at all and said: ' I have almost finished, Mr Konieczny, I am sorry but I cannot get to sleep when I am hungry.' He is quite right, I too cannot sleep when I am hungry, only after what had happened I could not eat at all, I kept seeing how they pulled the doctor out of the bathroom by his legs, in the morning the bathroom was clean, but after examining it carefully I discovered on the wall behind the tub a few small rusty spots – what is the value of human life? The famous and the great leave something behind them, but an ordinary man like myself when he is buried won't be remembered or missed by anyone except his nearest family, sometimes the family even feel relieved. That doctor must have suffered terribly if he chose that kind of death. I can't understand how a man with higher education gave no thought to the unpleasantness he would cause the staff of the clinic, the nurses and doctors, and most of all the Registrar, with whom they say he was on Christian name terms and thanks to whom he obtained a place here, although the clinic was full and they had to put an extra bed for him in the corridor. Everybody was very depressed this morning and it was so quiet in the corridors and wards as never before, Sister Yola told the Frenchman in confidence that the suicide's widow, if she wanted to, could bring a lawsuit against the clinic and call for an investigation, I know nothing about it, but I believe that if a man wants to commit suicide there is no way of preventing him, unless every step we take is to be watched and unless we are under observation day and night and the eyes of the watcher never leave us, but from my own experience I know how terrible it is and I would not wish such a misfortune on anyone, not even my worst enemy.

I wanted to say this to the Registrar when he asked me in
the passage how my work was progressing but I told him
that I don't find it easy, for I have no skill in writing and
therefore I should like to request him to be allowed to use
the psychologist's room until the end of the current week
and all through the following one, and then the Registrar
said: ' I wanted to talk to you about that very thing, Mr
Konieczny, because tomorrow or on Monday at the latest a
new patient will join us, a sociologist, we have agreed that
in his condition he should not change his normal way of life,
therefore we must give him an opportunity to continue his
ordinary work for three to four hours a day.' ' I understand,
Mr Registrar,' I said to him, ' I have a great respect for
knowledge and my case is very unimportant compared with
the achievements of scholars, it's like helpless David facing
mighty Goliath.' ' Don't talk rubbish, Mr Konieczny,' the
Registrar interrupted, 'no one has said that your case is unimportant, perhaps it is even more important than it seems
to you.' 'Thank you, Mr Registrar,' I bowed to him, ' I
know that you understand me and I shall be grateful to you
until the end of my days.' ' And do you know, Mr Konieczny, where I am going to stuff your gratitude?' he said. ' I
know, Mr Registrar,' I laughed, and this was the first time
for a long time that I have laughed.

He smiled too, but at once looked at me severely and said:
' If you know, pull yourself together and finish that letter
quickly, without going on too long, the sooner you finish it
and send it off, the better for you. Have you scribbled much
so far?' ' I believe so,' I said, ' but compared with all I want
to say, not enough.' 'Well then!' the Registrar said, ' go
on writing, but try to be concise. I suggest the following

arrangement to you: for the time being you may use the psychologist's room, in the evening after supper as well, but not later than up to nine pm, because you must relax before going to bed, and forget about everything.' 'It is not so easy, Mr Registrar,' I said and he said: 'If it were easy, I would not ask you to do it, is that clear?' 'I understand, Mr Registrar,' I said. 'Well then!' He tapped me on the shoulder. 'Go back to work; I give you until Sunday evening, say until Monday, but not longer, I cannot allow you to waste paper, a petition must be a petition, and not a novel in instalments. This time you must kindly leave out all flights of imagination.' He was going to walk away, but I stopped him and said: 'Mr Registrar, do you think the petition will help?' And then he looked at me and shouted: 'What do you think?' He screamed for all the world to hear: 'What do you take me for? You dare to assume that I am a doctor who would advise his patient to do futile and useless work? I resent the insinuation!' Oh, how grateful I am to him for having scolded me . . .

I was born on 1st May 1926 at the village of Kalety, district of Augustow, of parents – I am curious where they will find room for that sociologist, perhaps they will put him in the corridor too, unless somebody leaves before Saturday and a place becomes free in the ward, I will have to speak to him to find out if Alec could study sociology if he doesn't want to study law, I can't remember who it was, but somebody told me recently that very many famous sportsmen now study at the university, like Badenski the famous athlete and also two famous women runners, I forget their names, and many others, I will have to try and influence Alec while the boy is still ready to listen, I will also have to influence Halina, when I return home.

*

Evening of the same day

TO:

The Citizen First Secretary of the Polish United Workers' Party, Warsaw

PETITION

made by Marian Konieczny, technologist in the meat-products industry, domiciled at O, 17 Victory Avenue, Flat 5B, at present undergoing treatment in the Psychosomatic Clinic, City Hospital at T

I the undersigned earnestly request the Citizen First Secretary to consider personally the present petition and to give a just verdict so that the competent authorities should suspend the wrongful invigilation of my person and those guilty of breaking the law should be suitably punished and my full rights as a citizen should be restored to me in accordance with the Constitution of the People's Republic of Poland of July 1952.

I was born on 1st May 1926 at the village of Kalety, district of Augustow, of John and Aniela (née Kundicz) Konieczny, the youngest of six children. My father, of peasant origin, was employed as a forester in the forestry estate of Ciercierz, district of Augustow, and after the liberation was allotted five hectares of land in the village of Cierlica where he died in 1959. At the age of three, in 1929, I lost my mother, and myself and my brothers and sisters were brought up by my stepmother, Bronislawa (née

Kowalczyk) Konieczna, who died in 1943. By the outbreak
of the Second World War I had finished six classes of
primary school, after which for reasons beyond my control
I had to interrupt my schooling. In June 1943, I was
arrested by the Gestapo on suspicion of possessing hidden
arms and was taken to the Gestapo headquarters at Suwalki
where during three months of investigation I was subjected
to tortures, but although at the time I was a youth of barely
seventeen years old, I did not break down and did not betray anybody, although the arms I had hidden away be-
longed to my eldest brother, Alexander and I had known
that he was active in the underground. In September 1943
I was released from the Gestapo thanks to my aunt, Barbara Konieczna, who was employed as a housekeeper by
Father Matthew Borowicz, Rector of the parish of Ciercierz
– she bribed a Gestapo man who was an Austrian.

After my release, not feeling safe at home, in October
1943 I joined a group of partisans organized by the Polish
Insurgents' Union and active in the districts of Augustow
and Suwalki under the command of the Home Army. I
took part in many diversionary activities and in armed combat against punitive expeditions of the Wehrmacht. In
March 1944 I contracted typhoid and afterwards was ill
until November of that year, suffering in turn, among other
things, from pleurisy, oedema of the head and effusions
from the nose, for part of the time in the hospital at
Augustow and later, after our liberation by the Soviet
Armies, in my father's house.

In January 1945, I helped my uncle Wladyslaw
Konieczny to take over a farm that had been German-owned
in the hamlet of Karniewo, district of Elk, which my uncle

had been allotted within the framework of the resettlement action as compensation for the small-holding he had to move out of in the hamlet of Raczki, former district of Augustow.

In June 1945, when recruiting for the Citizens' Militia began, I answered the call and served for three years in the Militia, first at Augustow with the rank of Corporal, performing at Augustow at the same time the duties of Educational and Political Instructor, subseqently, from September 1947, as Commandant of the Militia post at Sokolany, district of Bialystok. I served throughout under harsh military conditions, not sparing my strength or my time to combat the gangs of the National Armed Forces, and to consolidate and strengthen the authority of People's Poland.

It must be ascribed to my youth and ideological and political immaturity that in June 1948 I was arrested by the Security Police and accused of having intimate relations with Citizen Yadwiga Kocik, who had become politically suspect because her brothers were found to be members of a Fascist group of the National Armed Forces – this was revealed when the youngest of them, Leszek Kocik (pseudonym Thunder) was captured in May 1948 and later sentenced to death, at which time it was further revealed that the second Kocik brother Andrew (pseudonym Wildcat) had been killed in a forest engagement in the autumn of 1947, while the third brother, Witold, had disappeared without trace. I did not know about all the foregoing until the arrest and unmasking of Leszek Kocik; Citizen Yadwiga Kocik swore that she was ignorant of her brothers' activities and did not maintain any contact with them. When I was arrested and held under investigation for seven months in the Security prison at Bialystok, I thought at first that I had been grievously wronged, only later, enlightened by the lieutenant in charge of investigations, I understood that as a member of the Citizens' Militia in the rank of commandant of a post, I was duty bound to be especially vigilant and had no right to excuse my actions by ignorance, so that I made my deposition in court in this spirit and when, in my last words, I pleaded guilty and asked for a just sentence, I was sentenced fairly to two-and-a-half years imprisonment and I served the above sentence in the prisons of Bialystok, Barczew and Ilawa. In the prison at Ilawa, on my own initiative and with the agreement and approval of the prison authorities, a circle for education in Marxist doctrine was formed, which allowed me to get better acquainted with revolutionary ideology; at Ilawa, too, I finished a trade course specializing in timber technology, so that my sojourn in prison, although it deprived me of my freedom, was beneficial to me and I left the prison more mature in mind, my health was undermined however by my having contracted TB which I had to have treatment for seven years later, as I have been suffering from it at various times. I had no difficulty in obtaining work after leaving prison, I was employed first in the District National Council at Mragow, in the Finance and Registry section, later in the Municipal National Council, in the Municipal Housing Management, and in both posts I worked fruitfully, never receiving any complaint from my superiors.

In 1953, desiring to develop a broader civic activity, I organized at O a Transport Co-operative and succeeded in enrolling in it almost all the people who owned vehicles in the town and its environs and who until then had worked on their own. As a reward for my social and organizational achievements I was nominated in 1954, with the agreement of the Provincial Committee of the Polish United Workers' Party, to the post of manager of the Cane-Panel and Pre-Fabricated One-Family House factory at Wilkasy. I devoted myself to these new duties and responsibilities with the utmost enthusiasm and energy, the more so because I had become a family man the previous year, having married Halina Tomaszewska, daughter of a railway official and works foreman, and on 19th February 1954 our first son, Alexander, was born.

All my efforts and endeavours were in vain, I have always desired to be efficient in the sector of activity entrusted to me but my honest desires were soon turned against me. I have been grievously wronged, Citizen First Secretary, being repaid as I have for all my efforts, and this happened when Director Gwiazda arrived from the head-office in Warsaw and I don't know whether somebody unfriendly to me had informed against me but from the very start of his inspection he seemed prejudiced and critical of me, also of my activities in my managerial post and of the methods I thought it right to apply in order to improve discipline and productivity at work, also the moral and ideological standards of my fellow-workers.

I, personally, contrary to what was held against me at the meeting of the workers, have never had a boss-mania, nor a swollen head, I have never broken the rule of law and never derived any personal benefits from my position, I only wanted my enterprise to exceed the plan not only to fulfil it and this is why, in my wish for improvement of the efficiency of our work, with the help of a few people devoted to me, I began to collect personal details concerning my subordinates that were relevant to their work, such as the style of their life outside working hours; I was led to do so by the correct Marxist premise that if one wants to raise people to a higher level one must have a clear picture of their characters. Later on, on the basis of these documents found by Director Gwiazda and read by him in public at a meeting of the workers, strong indictments against me were made and it was even said that I should be driven away from the factory in a barrow, but it did not come to this undeserved humiliation, probably my powerful enemies in the Counter-intelligence did not wish such a fate for me, although I am sure that they already had my long road of suffering mapped out; I have no proof that Director Gwiazda, when exposing me to shame, scorn and ridicule did not act on his own behalf, nor that the initiator of the whole compaign was not another person acting behind Gwiazda's back – in any case after that horrible meeting at which a resolution was unanimously passed condemning my activity for alleged cliquishness, dictatorial aspirations, and even for betraying the principles of Socialist morality, I made the irrevocable decision to resign the post of manager. Because I was very conscious of the wrong I had suffered and the misunderstanding of my intentions, I thought to myself that under the circumstances those who were to come after me must not benefit from my hard work, for if I had been a bad manager, probably everything initiated by me was bad, so in order that nothing should remain after me, in the presence of my brother-in-law, Citizen Victor Tomaszewski, also employed at the factory as specialist mycologist, I took from my desk a folder with development plans, made on my instructions by my deputy for technical affairs, Engineer

Casimir Borsuk and, still in my brother-in-law's presence, carried this folder to a room in which I occasionally slept when working late into the night and there, so that nothing should remain after me, I tore and burned the papers and by that action, which I performed in great sorrow and distress, I brought upon myself a terrible misfortune.

Only much later, after eight years, did I understand that my enemies, once they had marked me as their victim, were only waiting for an occasion to pounce on me and sink me, and I was providing such an occasion for them with my own hands. I must point out that after I had destroyed these development plans in October 1955, I was not summoned to the Security Office and no Security Officer ever spoke to me about it, only the Personnel Officer of the factory held a conversation with me about the above matter and I might easily have concealed the whole incident because Citizen Borsuk when I told him what I had done was completely unconcerned and declared that no harm had been done because he had a copy, but I did not want to lie and on leaving the factory told them the whole truth – this caused the people who were hostile to me at the workers' meeting to begin a campaign and make various accusations and gossip about me, I only understood later that my persecutors had planned it all from the start and foresaw everything with precision – I may not be very important, I am an average citizen, so I cannot be the butt of a great campaign, but THEY, once having selected such an ordinary citizen as victim, understand very well that it is not worth their while to destroy a small pawn with a lot of noise, it is enough to torture him by small but incessant pin-pricks while preserving a semblance of legality all the time, in order to drive that ordinary individual into a blind alley and make him submissive – but as I don't wish to capitulate and continue to demand justice, they are very bitter against me and won't let me out of their clutches, they would leave me alone if I allowed myself to be broken and made a false deposition, admitting my guilt and offences I did not commit, for God be my witness I have never been an agent of any foreign intelligence, I don't know the password they keep asking me for and have never known it – for that reason I have not passed on any information to anyone concerning the personnel of the Cane-Panel and Pre-Fabricated One-Family House factory at Wilkasy nor handed the development plans of the above-mentioned factory to any person not entitled to see them, because I destroyed the original and have a witness in the person of my brother-in-law, Citizen Victor Tomaszewski, but people have been unwilling to believe his testimony because of our kinship, and have ganged up against me, although earlier on I had done all right by them, subsequently they did not have a good word to say for me, I became a black sheep, a social outcast. I might have done better to have given everything up and disappeared from sight, to have gone somewhere far away, to Lower Silesia, to Szczecin, or Zielona Góra, but it was difficult for me to leave my part of the country, where I had spent my childhood and youth and my first adult years, and as I felt innocent, I could not reconcile myself to voluntary exile with my wife and child. I say this now, because at the time, as I have mentioned, I did not have a full understanding that wherever I escaped, wherever my homeless wanderings took me, to the western or northern areas, to a provincial capital, or to any God-forsaken settlement, THEY would soon have tracked me down, for the cruel sentence had been passed on me and it was not in my competence to alter my terrible fate. I cannot conceive now how I could have been so blind and deaf at that time and for the eight years that followed, but perhaps my lack of discernment can be justified by the circumstances that feeling pure as the driven snow I was able to understand the evil talk which has caused me so much suffering, and made me so angry, but I could not imagine the extent of the conspiracy against me, the ruthlessness of its methods or its cruel and highly illegal purpose. So, unaware of the essence of the problem, I began to look round for another job, because my own livelihood and my family's were seriously threatened, and for that reason I accepted the first offer that came along and began to work on the State agricultural estate at Swiatki, as store-keeper, in a cattle breeding unit. But from the start I had great difficulties in the execution of my duties, for although our unit supplied fodder to several other units in the area we had no weighbridge and each transport of fodder had to be assessed on sight, and therefore various shortages occurred and when, as a result of insufficient feeding, the cattle and horses began to die in our unit's distribution area, the authorities stepped in and I as storekeeper was arrested, but during interrogation my innocence became obvious, because I had been forced by circumstances to be inaccurate and it was not me but the others who derived benefit from that fact. I do not exclude another eventuality, namely that during that investigation, although innocent, I might have received a sentence if my powerful enemies, who had other intentions towards me, had not whispered a word where necessary and persuaded the prosecutor to suspend proceedings against me. I don't maintain that this is definitely how it was, but it might have been.

I was released from arrest at Swiatki in November 1957; I have forgotten to mention that while I was discharging my duties as storekeeper on the State agricultural estate at Swiatki, my wife gave birth in December 1955 to my second son John, and when I was arrested she was pregnant again, and this is why, no sooner had I been discharged, although I had a recurrence of TB as a result of all my experiences, and was not at all fit, I began to look feverishly for work. This time I was lucky, because I met by chance an acquaintance who had been my colleague in the Citizens' Militia at Augustow, Citizen Richard Kuna – we were detailed together in 1946 to help organize the People's Referendum – and it transpired that he was an important man, the Chairman of the State Co-operative of Food Producers at Lidzbark, so when we met after all those years he understood my situation, and as he knew only the best about me, he at once gave me a job in the Food Producers' Co-operative as deputy manager of the butchery, on condition that before taking on the job, I would be given sick leave. I took advantage of this and spent six weeks at Polanica-Spa; that rest improved my health considerably and since then I have not had a recurrence of TB.

After my return from treatment, I began work on 1st February 1958 at the Food Producers' Co-operative at Lidzbark, province of Olsztyn.

During my employment there until 31st July 1963, I was the first among the workers, no reward ever passed me by, every opportunity, every holiday was a reward for my work and so it continued until 1963. Because of housing difficulties, I had to travel six kilometres to work. During that time I also studied as an external student at Lodz, at the Food Producers Technical College, but in spite of the difficulties of supporting a family of five, including three small children, travelling to work by various means of transport and every fortnight making a train journey of five hundred kilometres to college in Lodz, I did not break down and carried my burdens without a word of complaint. I couldn't help noticing however, all the time, that something was secretly happening around me, this did astonish me, but my aim was to work and provide for my family.

The beginning of 1963 brought radical changes, because the organized campaign against me broke out into the open. My health began to suffer and in April 1963, feeling undermined in my will to live and in my spirit as a result of the campaign, I declared to the Chairman of the State Food Producers' Co-operative, Citizen Richard Kuna, that I was unable to cope with the situation in the section under my control and Citizen Richard Kuna replied that he knew this; yet in spite of my bad state of health I continued working until 14th July 1963, although I was completely broken in spirit. In May 1963, after a conversation with Chairman Citizen Richard Kuna, seeing that the campaign around me had not ceased and being in a bad state of health, I unwittingly asked to be released from my job and was answered with three months' notice and my work contract dissolved as from 31st July 1963, while on 19th July that year my health broke down completely: my sister Yadwiga Konieczna, employed in the Bishop's Curia at T, took me under her care, and thanks to her help I was admitted to the Psychosomatic Clinic of the City Hospital at T, under the

THE APPEAL

care of Registrar Dr Stefan Plebanski. My name was black-
ened, both in the local community and with my nearest
family, and I became a social outcast.

In hospital at T, thanks to good medical care I was somewhat restored to mental stability, the treatment lasted for
two months, later I went at my own expense to Naleczow,
for convalescent leave of three weeks, and thus I reached
31st December 1963 on doctors' certificates. I was laughed
at, people said I had become a lunatic, that this was the end
of me and I would starve, my enemies from the Counter-
intelligence began to act more and more shamelessly, sending spies and agents against me who acted singly, or sometimes, for better effect, organized themselves in pairs or
threes, and wherever I showed myself in the street or a
public place they aped me, making malicious gestures so
that I should break down completely and mention the password, and some of their tricks must have been dictated to
them by the Electronic Brain, for in certain situations I was
alone and no one could see me, yet this too was no secret
to them, so that I lived under continuous pressure, knowing
that their devilish eyes could see me at every moment, all
the same I told myself that I wouldn't let myself be
harassed to the extent of admitting to crimes I had not
committed.

On 1st January 1964 I began work at the Lidzbark
Provincial Wholesale Food Products Enterprise, at the
wholesale depot, I was given the post of Senior Executive
in the depot, salary 1,300 zloty a month, I was swamped
with work, had to come to work at five am, at three pm I
was brought a pile of orders and told to have them ready
for 6.30 am the next morning for distribution, otherwise the

transport would be idle, the Director Citizen Jezierski said so and he advised me to work overtime, so I did not take any notice of anything although the campaign continued behind my back, I was being teased like a dog, but in spite of this I continued work until 14th January 1964 inclusive: on that day I again broke down and on 15th January 1964 I did not go to work, but stayed sick at home: on 16th January 1964 a driver of a light lorry from Lidzbark came to my house and declared that Citizen Jezierski had sent him to enquire why Citizen Konieczny had not reported for work for two days, to which my wife answered that I was sick and had gone to a doctor at Lidzbark, for indeed I went to see a doctor on 16th January 1964, and on 17th January 1964 I went on doctor's orders to the Provincial Mental Health Out-Patients Clinic at Olsztyn, there I was examined by a board at 5.30 pm, on 18th January 1964 I bought the prescribed medicine 'Tofrenil' at Olsztyn and then I returned home on 19th January 1964 which was a Sunday, so only on 20th January 1964 was my wife able to take to my place of work the doctor's certificate which was a recommendation for a fortnight's sick leave from 15th January until 31st January 1964, but Director Jezierski did not pay any attention to it, he concealed the fact that the driver of the light lorry had been to my house and I was sacked from work in accordance with the instructions of my enemies. This caused another breakdown so that on 21st January 1964 I was forced to go again to T for a second stay in the Psychosomatic Clinic, and there I again spent two months which improved my health a lot. At first, though, as previously I was persecuted by the Counter-intelligence, which – by threats and bribes – kept selecting agents from among the staff and the patients who kept an eye on me all the time and aped me continuously, later this ceased when they realized that I had pulled myself together after having regained some strength. At the end of March 1964 I returned home, but I could not find any work and support of the family fell on my wife's shoulders, so to save money and fares to her work we moved to O to a room sub-let to us in his flat by my brother-in-law, Citizen Victor Tomaszewski, who had also been recruited by the Counter-intelligence, but we had no other way out. My wife is always being promised a temporary flat, for the co-operative one is not to be finished till 1969, and so we have to suffer all together, and there is no end of this torture in sight, and so, Citizen First Secretary, if you won't consider my petition justly and won't give me a helping fatherly hand while the campaign against me continues, I should prefer the hand of the enemy to give me a final blow so that I won't rise again, but they darcn't take such a step, they have allotted me long-term torture. So from sheer despair at being excluded from social, political and economic life and burdened with such terrible accusations, although I am pure as the driven snow, in September 1967 my nervous condition deteriorated so much that I found myself in a state of crisis for the third time and had to go to T to the Psychosomatic Clinic. Now I am well and calm, but the prospect of what is awaiting me after my return home robs me of any zest for life and in you, Citizen First Secretary, is my only hope, please restore me to the Motherland, to People's Poland, also help my wife and children, for they are suffering innocently for the fact that their husband and father has become a social outcast. I thank you from the depths of my heart and commend

43

myself once again to your justice and await an answer to the above address,

Yours faithfully,

Marian Konieczny

PS   I have been a member of a Trade Union since I began to work, i.e. for fifteen years, also a member of the Popular Party, but I have been pushed out of any broader social, political and economic life since I have been under suspicion, which hurts me enormously as a Pole and a patriot of the Political Order for which I have fought.

*

On Friday, during the usual hours of the afternoon, Konieczny wrote:

In the morning, immediately after the doctors' round, I showed the Registrar all that I wrote yesterday to ask his advice whether I have composed a correct petition and I was very astonished that a few hours later, before dinner, the Registrar summoned me, looked at me sternly but humorously as he knows how to do, and said: 'Do you know what I thought, Mr Konieczny, while reading your lucubration? I thought that when you occupied managerial posts you must have plagued your subordinates with long speeches – did you, Mr Konieczny?' I did not feel embarrassed and answered: 'Yes, indeed, it did happen sometimes as you say, Mr Registrar, I cannot hide anything from you, the fact is that sometimes I used to speak for an hour and more, but only when the situation required it and when there were many matters to point out and discuss, because

44

it has always been my aim to explain a problem from as many sides as possible and against the background of the given situation, but does that mean that my petition is no good?' 'No,' said the Registrar, 'it is a little long, you dwell unnecessarily on secondary details, but generally speaking it is all right, you must now copy it and we shall send it where you want to send it.' 'All right, Mr Registrar,' I said, 'I will copy it immediately today, thank you, sir,' and when I rose to go, I remembered what I had thought about before falling asleep the previous night, so I said: 'I am sorry, Mr Registrar, but I have one doubt, I remembered last night that at the beginning I said "Petition" – it crossed my mind that perhaps it would be better to write ' "Appeal", what is your opinion, Mr Registrar?' He again looked at me, but this time without humour, and said: "Appeal"? and why do you assume that "appeal" will be better than "petition"?' I didn't quite know what to answer, so I said: 'For if I am innocent, Mr Registrar, I am not a petitioner to the Citizen First Secretary and don't ask him for justice, but I appeal to him as the highest authority in People's Poland for my legal position to be restored.' 'You are right, Mr Konieczny,' said the Registrar, 'copy your Appeal now.' For this reason I spent the whole afternoon working in the psychologist's room, but was unable to finish, so, with the Registrar's authorization, I went back to work after supper and now, at 7.35 pm I have this work behind me and don't even feel tired, only I don't know whether I have done it well, I don't agree with the Registrar that I have given too many details, on the contrary I consider that in many points I have been too concise and consequently omitted many important factors, or presented them without sufficient clarity, so I have decided that of course I will prepare a fair copy of the Appeal for despatch, (although it came to fifteen and a half foolscap pages), as the Registrar wishes, but just in case it should prove that supplements are necessary, I shall continue to work, if I can't have the psychologist's room then in the corridor or on my bed, it doesn't matter where because, should these supplements become necessary or be asked for by Citizen First Secretary, I must be prepared to supply them at once in any given quantity.

Today at dinner (we had potato soup, then fried cod with potatoes and spinach, and stewed apples for pudding) an unpleasant thing happened and later I became very restless, but this is over now – it is obvious however that my nerves are not quite strong yet, therefore I must watch myself carefully to maintain a proper attitude in the next few days. With the exception of breakfast when there is PT in the corridor, we have all our meals there and sit at a table in the same company as we sleep. I don't know whether I have acted rightly, but from the very beginning I have not concealed what I worked on in the afternoon in the psychologist's room, so at almost every supper when I come downstairs, either the Colonel or the Frenchman asks me in a friendly way how the work is going, and I tell them how it has gone. I didn't really notice until today that only Raphael has never asked any questions before – he has always listened attentively, yes, but not taken part in the conversation, and I didn't use to pay any attention to this, as it seemed quite natural to me that a young boy shouldn't interfere in talk about such delicate matters, so that it struck me at once when today it was not the Colonel or the Frenchman (he

THE APPEAL

wants to leave the clinic but the Registrar is against it) but
Raphael who was the first to ask how the work had gone.

I at once noticed that he looked at me with a smile which
seemed friendly, but which was also slightly mocking as if
he wanted me to understand that he knew more than he was
prepared to say – a shiver ran down my spine because
Raphael's remark and his smile seemed suspect to me, but
I took hold of myself and calmly explained that I had finished the essential work yesterday and that the Registrar
had approved it, so today I was making a fair copy, but
no sooner did I say this than it crossed my mind: why say
it, why betray myself, he knows that I put my exercise book
in a cardboard folder with my documents, and that I place
this under my pillow – if I should leave the room for a minute
to go to the toilet, in my absence he might steal all my hard
work, destroy it or send it somewhere, or even if he didn't
steal it so as not to unmask himself, he might inform them
what I had been doing and how far I have gone. 'Have you
no appetite today, Mr Konieczny?' I heard the Frenchman ask; he had just returned from the kitchen with a
second helping of potato soup. 'No, I haven't,' I said, 'I
am a little tired today.' 'You work too much,' said the
Colonel, and the Frenchman added that some red wine
would not come amiss to celebrate the completion of my
work.

I didn't say anything, only stealthily kept observing
Raphael, but he seemed normal, like any other day, and
asked the Colonel who always reads *The People's Tribune*
about the television programme in the evening, so I thought
that I must have imagined things, I was overtired and that
was why my nerves were tense.

It isn't likely that they should make use of such a young boy, but if people are unscrupulous in their methods anything may happen, during my previous stays in the clinic many different things happened, they had various agents here, even tried to organize pairs and threes among the patients to keep me permanently under observation, but lately I haven't detected any signs of their activities in the clinic, though none are necessary really, it might even suit them to know that I was getting better and my nerves were stronger so that they could pounce on me more openly and torture me, but now, I thought, a new situation had arisen and if they had detected what I was doing with the help of the Electronic Brain, and what my plans were, they might be anxious that I would unmask them before the Highest Authority – so they speedily found a spy among the patients – a half-grown boy probably caught their attention, he is observant like all boys of his age, and as he is under age, he wouldn't be suspected. It wouldn't be difficult to tempt and bribe a boy like that by promising him that should he have any difficulty at school – and Raphael is in his second year of the Technical Electrical College at Pulawy – they would see to it that he didn't lose a year, he said himself that he had difficulties with his studies. This is what I thought and for a moment a terrible despair got hold of me that even here in this refuge there is no security for me, so with a heavy heart I asked: 'I hear that you are to leave us soon, Raphael?' and he smiled pleasantly and nicely: 'Oh yes,' he said, 'Dr Plebanski told me that I will leave next Wednesday,' and at once added: 'On Sunday I'll get a pass to go out, because my uncle is coming here.'

When he smiled, my doubts disappeared, but when he

mentioned that pass, I again began to wonder if he wouldn't go out in fact to contact his employers and find out what information he is to collect and pass on to them. After supper I didn't lie down to rest before work in the psychologist's room, but checked if the exercise book was in its place and then went out into the corridor and positioned myself next to the bathroom so that Raphael couldn't see me, but I could see him enter the dormitory – he didn't go there, immediately after supper he went to watch television and this calmed me a lot and I was able to work in peace all evening, and now I am still calm, but very tired, I must have imagined things with Raphael, my nerves ran away with me, the Lord would not let me be humiliated at every step, worse than Job.

*

On Saturday, still under the influence of the after-dinner conversation between the Colonel and the Frenchman, when after a renewed discussion of the doctor's suicide they went on to talk about the astonishing mysteries of the world and the cosmos, Konieczny spent about two hours in the psychologist's room, musing over his open exercise book; he thought among other things of the incredibly vast galaxies rushing through space with dizzy speed sometimes approaching half the speed of light, he pondered a moment on the size of the heavenly bodies billions of times larger than earth and on starlight that reaches us after billions of years when the stars themselves, cold or extinguished, had ceased to shine before life began on our planet and when it was a ball of fire whirling in the darkness of the cosmos; and immediately after thinking this he pricked up his ears because out of the chaotic and bewildering conversation he remembered that the room in which he was sitting alone and generally every spot on earth was filled with hundreds of thousands of radio waves, long, medium, short and ultra-short, as if every square yard of space were ready, at the touch of a magic wand, to resound with thousandfold tunes and voices, which however, when no one or nothing summons them, float invisibly by in dead silence. And what about the mysterious waves, not yet analysed by scientists, which the human brain probably sends out and receives? Here he shivered slightly, broke out in a sweat at the temples, and his right leg began to rock more intensively under the desk, because in this respect he knew more than many other people, even a hundred times more educated and intelligent than himself. Who but himself had had the occasion and the misfortune to experience personally and completely the ominous power of the electronic machine installed by his enemies to watch and record every one of his steps and thoughts? So in the face of an enemy conjured up so unexpectedly, his instinct of self-preservation ordered him to retreat speedily into the depths of the oceans, that strange and little known area of watery darkness and silence, full of mysterious life and natural riches; he imagined that he was resting in the deep of an ocean bed under swirling mountains of waters, and then he tried to visualize the wanderings of eels, the mass movements of tribes of fishes from the centre of the land mass, from lakes and muddy streams, wanderings for millions of generations directed unerringly towards the distant spawning grounds somewhere in the Atlantic Ocean named the Sargasso Sea, to end their lives after the mating season, and to pass on to their progeny the route to their native waters; in a more distant perspective, he imagined the rush of the vast waters of death and the new life; later he soared like a cosmonaut, flying to the stars and for a moment hung in the emptiness and darkness of boundless cosmic space, where on a scale incomprehensible to the human mind the largest stars seem no larger than miscroscopic specks of dust. Who or rather what is man and what is the meaning and reason for his short sojourn on earth, on this astonishingly small planet turning round its own axis, and together with other planets circling round the red-hot and perpetually exploding sun and finally, together with the whole solar system, rushing as part of a powerful galaxy with giddy speed into the unknown – where? for how long? and most of all why? What is the purpose of that mad movement, that inhuman precipitation, that circling, like the agitation of a swarm of flies in a missile shot into space? At last he felt so oppressed by his ignorance and his own smallness that he returned to his ward before five o'clock. But first he noted in his exercise book:

I would quietly close my eyes for ever if I were to live long enough to see my sons grown up and Alex a judge, Johnny an astronomer and Mickey a dancer in the Warsaw Opera, please God keep my sons under your gracious care . . .

*

In the evening of that Saturday, Konieczny began a new exercise book and on the first page wrote carefully:

ADDENDUM

to my Appeal directed to Citizen

First Secretary of the Central Committee, Polish United Workers' Party, Warsaw

Then he continued as follows:

She was a decent girl, from the landowning family of Kocik, and she would have made a good wife, had not a higher force separated us. When I joined the Citizens' Militia at Augustow, I was allotted a billet with some people named Jedryczek, he had been a clerk in the Municipal Offices, or the former City National Council, but had been pensioned off when I met them. They had a bungalow with a garden in Marchlewski Street, formerly 11th November Street – when I got my billet there, they at first looked at me askance, later less so, they even seemed pleased to have a uniformed official in the house, for times were uncertain, they only feared that because of my presence they might be attacked at night by an armed gang, but when I began to give them some of my rations and some supplementary coupons they calmed down and we lived together peacefully thereafter. I used my room very little, for sometimes I had to be on duty for two or three nights in a row.

It was through Citizen Wanda Jedryczek that I met Yadwiga Kocik, her god-daughter, when she came to Augustow from Sokolany where she lived with her mother, the widow of an NCO in the Polish Army killed in September 1939. Yadwiga was employed as a waitress at Sokolany in a café in Joseph Stalin Square, and on her day off she came to Augustow to do some shopping and call on her godmother, and it so happened that I too had a day off, so I met her there and we fell in love at first sight. I have never met a girl like her either before or since, it was not that she was particularly pretty, she was dark-haired and she had sad and sombre eyes, but when she smiled you could see blue skies in those eyes, she was not talkative, but it was pleasant even to stay silent with her, we did not need words, I could guess her thoughts and she could guess mine without any words because our hearts beat with one feeling – later when fatal circumstances clouded our love and I felt that misfortune was approaching with long strides, we hardly spoke at all when we were together, and we were happy although very sad – once, I remember, when we were lying in the dark she reached for my hand, pressed it hard and said to me: 'Marian, I shall never forgive myself for bringing such a misfortune upon your head,' my throat then felt terribly tight, but I answered: 'Yadwiga, my beloved, whatever happens to us, I shall give thanks to God to the end of my days that I have known you and I trust that everything will still turn out for the best and that we'll always live together.'

This did not happen, alas, for when I was released from prison, I lost all trace of her, she and her mother went to prison too, but for a short time, and I learned much later that Citizen Maria Kocik died in the late autumn of 1949 and Yadwiga soon afterwards left Sokolany and went to the Szczecin district, so people said, but I couldn't find out precisely where, it was difficult for me to start a search, because after leaving prison I had to have treatment for TB which I had contracted there, then I took a job and so hard life extinguished the beautiful flame of my youth, I don't even know if she's alive, and if so where she is now and how her life has turned out, I assume that she must have found a husband and has a family, good luck to her – it is better for her that we have not met again and that fate has taken her out of my blighted life, she would not have had a happy life with me – Oh no! – and as it is I have a few beautiful memories to cherish and she, I hope, does not remember me too badly, if she remembers me at all.

I remember, that first day we met, when she had to go back to Sokolany, I offered to take her to the bus stop but she refused to let me and although I felt disappointed I did not insist, out of politeness, and when afterwards I felt rather depressed at home, old Mrs Jedryczek said: 'It is because of your uniform, Marian,' because she had grown fond of me and addressed me by my Christian name. 'Why because of the uniform?' I said in great surprise, 'It is an official uniform, it is not disgraceful to wear it.' 'Disgraceful or not,' she answered, 'I am too old to discuss politics but maybe a young girl does not like to show herself to people in such company.' I was a little angry: 'What are you saying, Mrs Jedryczek?' I exclaimed, 'I am a representative of the Government,' but when I quietened down I thought that perhaps she had spoken the truth, and in fact when I met Yadwiga more than six months later for the second time, this was at Sokolany, she blushed like a rose when she saw me, because she did not know yet that I had been transferred to the Militia post there.

I heard from Mrs Jedryczek that whenever she came to Augustow when I was on duty, she always asked about me, so when during our second meeting we were walking a little way toward Stalin Square, I asked: 'Is it true that you did not wish me to take you to the bus stop at Augustow because I was wearing Militia uniform?' She walked in silence by my side for a few minutes, then she said: 'You know that from my godmother?' 'You've guessed,' I replied, and she said: 'It's true, and I am sorry for it.' It was unpleasant to hear it, but pleasant too at the same time. 'Why are you apologizing to me, Miss Yadwiga?' I said, 'It is I who should apologize to you for having been indelicate, I know that all kinds of people work in the Militia, even hostile individuals have penetrated its ranks, there are those, too, who abuse their power, and those who benefit personally from the service, but one must not judge from exceptional cases that everybody is the same, am I not right, Miss Yadwiga?' 'You are a decent man,' she said, 'you say what you think and I respect you for it.' 'Do you only respect me, Miss Yadwiga?' I asked. 'Is that too little?' she said, and I don't know how I had the boldness to say it for until then I had had little to do with women, it must have been my love that caused me to say: 'From anybody else I would not ask for more, but from you it is too little.' She did not answer and we continued our walk in silence until she said: 'It is a lovely day, don't you think so, Mr Marian?' I felt speechless with great emotion and only after a while could I answer: 'Thank you, Miss Yadwiga,' and again we fell silent but felt at ease with one another, because she had an exceptional character for a woman, she never said an unnecessary word, and when she said something, it was from the depths of her soul.

It is not her fault, poor girl, that her own brothers were Fascist bandits, it was a terrible tragedy. I have always believed that the hostile and criminal activities of her brothers were unknown to her, she may have guessed that something was wrong, her mother must have known something, but I would swear that Yadwiga did not, and generally speaking the fact that they did not murder her for going out with me and not concealing it at all was a real miracle, the brothers probably didn't shoot her because my presence served as a screen, for who could have suspected that the brothers of a Militiaman's girl were members of a forest gang, active in the same area, murdering our people and assassinating our officials? Until the moment when Thunder, that is Leszek Kocik, was caught with a gun in his hands and sent to be interrogated, I had no suspicions, I knew that Yadwiga was not her mother's only child and had some brothers, but I was never interested in the matter, they had existed, now they had disappeared, like many people at the time who were lost or disappeared without trace. I kept silent so as not to ask any awkward questions and not to reopen old wounds, how should I have known what the truth was? Misfortune fell like a thunderbolt from a clear sky, and under the first impact of it I tried to make Yadwiga escape with me and start a new life with me somewhere in the Regained Territories, even under changed names, but she did not want to take the risk. I remember that she said to me: 'No, Marian, I want to be with you always, but if we did the thing you want us to, a bigger misfortune would befall us, now you will get a mild sentence, but if you deserted, you could be punished by death, Poland is not a desert, they would soon find us, no Marian, I cannot agree to your ruining your life, you still have the whole of it before you.' 'I don't want any life without you,' I said, for I really felt like that then, although I was barely twenty-two. 'You will forget.' 'Don't misjudge me, Yadwiga,' I said in despair, 'I will never never forget you, but I will do as you wish me to do, my heart is bleeding that fratricidal struggles have broken

and destroyed our happiness.' The officer of the Security
Service who was interrogating me said one day: 'I know,
Konieczny, that until Thunder's arrest you did not know
anything about Miss Kocik's brothers, but this does not relieve you from responsibility, because your fault and your
offence lies in the fact that you did not know. If you think
correctly about the whole matter, Konieczny, and you will
have plenty of time to do so, you will come to the conclusion
that you should be grateful to us for having released you
from the Militia and arrested you. There were some com-
rades – why deny it? – who wanted you to be left alone
until you would become "ripe", which means that after
learning about everything you would still continue to see
Miss Kocik and in such a case you would have to be accused
under another paragraph of the Code, do you understand
me, Konieczny?' 'Yes, Citizen Lieutenant,' I said, because
I realized then what a terrible abyss I might have fallen
into. 'Well then,' he said, 'we finally decided that this
would be a pity, you are young, at a small cost we might
make a valuable individual of you, we won't give you much,
two or three years at most, but you must remember in court,
first, to show contrition that, being a member of the Citizens' Militia, you did not show sufficient vigilance, so you
must plead guilty; secondly, to admit frankly how things
were and that Miss Kocik consciously misled you, concealing from you the truth about her brothers who were
bandits.' I thought I had misheard him. 'How is that, Citizen Lieutenant, that would be a false deposition, because
I can swear on everything that is holy and dear to me that
she did not know about anything, she is an honest girl.'
'An honest girl, you say?' said he. 'Well then, if she were

as honest as you say, she should have been loyal to you and have had no secrets from you, this would be common sense, and if this were so, you would have to answer not for negligence and dereliction of duty, but for knowingly having concealed the activities of the brothers Kocik. What is more: if you, a commandant of a Militia post, had concealed such a thing from the authorities, you must yourself have gone over to the enemy and have had contacts with the bandits, for in whose interest would you be helping them? This is how matters stand in the light of your actual deposition, we are sorry for you, Konieczny, for you are digging your own grave, perhaps you don't fully realize what you have said? Think about it, we shall have a talk again tomorrow, consider everything calmly.' I felt very frightened that I'd have another twenty-four hours of terrible thinking to do, so I said: 'May I ask a question, Citizen Lieutenant?' 'Fire away,' he said. 'Assuming, Citizen Lieutenant,' I said, 'that I shall make a depositon in court as you wish me to – ' He immediately interrupted me: 'You are to tell the truth and not what I wish you to say.' 'Yes, of course, Citizen Lieutenant,' I said, 'but what proof can I give the court that she had known about the gang activities of her brothers?' He looked at me attentively and said: 'Don't you worry about that, Konieczny, your duty is to tell the truth, leave the rest to the court.' 'Yes, of course, Citizen Lieutenant,' I said.

I liked that lieutenant, because I have got accustomed to the military style and he probably also felt that there was no enmity in me, quite the contrary, for after a moment he said: 'Listen, Konieczny, I understand that it is not easy to accuse one's own girl-friend before the court, but just think what uniform you have been wearing and what oath you have taken, do you remember?' 'Yes, Citizen Lieutenant,' I said, 'I remember.' 'Well then!' he added after a while: 'And in court your word will be sufficient if your attitude is correct, the court won't have any reason not to believe you, we mistrust only our enemies and you, Konieczny, are not an enemy.' 'No, Citizen Lieutenant,' I said, 'I am not an enemy, I have never been one.' Therefore, after thinking it over, I agreed to testify as conditions of the class struggle demanded, but I am comforted by the knowledge that this fact did not harm Yadwiga, because she was released after less than a year's investigation, her mother was kept in prison a little longer, but she too was released and died a free woman. During that time, I was plagued by one thought: what would happen if there was a confrontation with Yadwiga in court, but the lieutenant assured me that such a confrontation did not have to take place, my word would be enough and so it was, luckily for Yadwiga and myself, for I don't know what I would have said if I had seen my Yadwiga as a witness in the box, perhaps I would have broken down, but even so I would not have helped Yadwiga in her misfortune, for a dangerous disrepute would have fallen upon her, poor girl, if in the light of objective truth I were made to appear as an enemy of People's Poland, and as it happened she was only interrogated about having maintained contact with her brothers and in the end they had to accept the facts, because her case did not reach the court. She must have suffered a lot, poor thing, but what was there to be done? Times were difficult and every citizen had to carry the burden of suffering. I myself began to understand many things only during investigation and later in prison, because I have improved my mind, learned a lot ideologically, and have matured.

*

On Sunday afternoon Konieczny continued to work in the psychologist's room on his 'Addendum'. He wrote:

My brothers and sisters. Of the six children that survived – Zbigniew born in 1916, having died of diphtheria in early childhood and the youngest one Witold having died together with my mother during her confinement in 1929 – only five are alive, but apart from my sister Barbara, employed in the Bishop's Curia at T who came to my assistance when misfortune struck me, it is as if I had no brothers or sisters at all, each of them has gone his own way, although they have the same mother and father. The eldest, christened Alexander after our grandfather, Alexander Kundicz, was arrested in September 1944, when I was dangerously ill with typhoid, he was deported to the East and has never been heard of again, probably he is no longer alive, a great pity because he was a man of great character, he didn't owe it to anyone else when he finished secondary school, later he graduated with honours from the Polytechnic High College in Warsaw, the only one of all the family to have obtained higher education, God rest his soul; it must have been hard for him to die so far from the Motherland and his nearest, he had a fiancée, Joanna was her name, I don't remember her surname, I never met her because she lived in Warsaw and that was where they met, I don't know what happened to her, perhaps she is not alive either. The second sister, Aniela, born in 1920, was deported to Germany for forced labour in the spring of 1942, she worked in a munitions factory near Hanover and was liberated by the Americans in 1944, she met a sergeant of Polish origin, married him and now lives in Detroit, but she seldom writes – she has drifted away from the family, for why should she care about our worries and sorrows when she's doing well, her children are probably completely American, she has her own house and a car, our little Angie's gone far since the days when she minded the cows and walked barefoot to school in the hamlet of Ciercierz, she could afford to send a parcel from time to time, at least for the children, but never mind – she's had a hard time too, working for the Nazis can't have been easy, I can't even remember the names of her children, she has a son and a daughter, probably some Billy or Betty or something like that, I am curious if they can speak Polish, probably not.

The third sister, Yadwiga, was born in 1922, she has also married, her husband is Engineer Andrew Kobiela, who works in the Boleslaw Bierut mines at Walbrzych. She came to see us a few times for Christmas or the summer holidays when my father was alive and lived at Cierlica, but she hasn't been back since my father's death in 1959. They're doing well, they can afford to go on holiday to the coast or to the mountains, my children have not seen any part of Poland except Mazury – the eldest, Alec, went once to a summer camp at Ustka, but when he came back he said he preferred Mazury and I agree that Mazury is the most beautiful part of Poland, although the regions of Augustow and Suwalki are also pretty and picturesque. I haven't been to home parts for a long time, me and my brother Stanislaw who is farming on my father's plot of land,

we are like strangers, or worse, politics divided us when I
was serving with the Citizens' Militia, he's doing quite well,
but has the soul of a kulak – I remember when I got two
days' leave for Christmas 1946 I went on my motorbike to
my father's, not minding the danger I was exposing myself
to, because there were many National Armed Forces bands
in the forests, and when I arrived unharmed, although I
was frozen stiff in spite of my sheepskin, there was twenty
degrees of frost and a strong wind, Staszek came out of the
cottage and said this to greet me, his brother: 'What are
you looking for here, no one will give you any Moscow
roubles here, get back to your Russkis.' I felt as if my face
had been slapped, for I had never taken roubles and have
served People's Poland in constant danger of my life, but
I took hold of myself and asked: 'Where is father?' And he
said: 'You'd better tell me where Alexander is, and I'll tell
you where father is.' I understood that I was not wanted, for
father must have been turned against me as well so without
a word I started to go away and out of their sight forever,
when Staszek must have thought better of it, his conscience probably moved him, or perhaps he was afraid I'd
make life unpleasant for him, for he called after me and
when I stopped he said: 'You have nothing to be offended
for, truth hurts, but also cures, and as today is the anniversary of Our Lord Jesus's birth, one must not deny hospitality even to the worst criminal, so come in if you wish.' I
did not go in, not because I was offended or angry, I only
thought that one can't accept hospitality when one feels
forced to do so and that no Holy Day can resuscitate love
which is dead, so I said: 'I don't wish to be your guest, and
as to Our Lord Jesus's birthday I can spend this holiday

any place, even on my motorbike, the Lord Jesus knows my thoughts and actions, he knows that there is no treason or corruption in them.' After leaving Cierlica on that Christmas Eve, I didn't see my brother Stanislaw for a long time, I was told he was pleased when I was sent to prison and said I needed to be taught a lesson, perhaps I would become wiser and my eyes would open to the downfall and subjection of our nation. It wasn't till 1959, when my father died, that I went to Cierlica again for the funeral – my brother didn't make any remarks, he was even quite polite, but there was no brotherly feeling left between us, he was like a stranger to me and I was one to him, if my mother had been alive she would have suffered at such a rift between her children, father probably as well, were it not for the fact that he, poor man, spent the last years of his life deprived of speech and understanding, for in the winter of 1956 he had a stroke which left him paralysed until the end of his days.

The above is the history of my sisters and brothers born of the same parents, but scattered by the winds of destiny all over the world, and strangers to one another. I rather envy families who gather round an old mother and father in love and respect at a table together, at Christmas or Easter, grandchildren sitting side by side with their grandparents, and parents living in happy marital union. I often wonder what my children will be like when they grow up, will they be united by brotherly love and cherish their parents in love and gratitude, or will each of them fly away from the parental nest in a different direction and never look back at what they have left behind? Of all my brothers and sisters I think most often about Alexander, he was an

intelligent and big-hearted man, he would certainly understand my misfortune and provide me with good advice and
support me with a brotherly shoulder, but he is nowhere on
this earth now and I can only pray for him sometimes,
although he probably doesn't need any prayers because he
will have gone to Heaven anyway.

Sunday evening
I had a difficult character, I was jumpy and easily aroused,
I shouted and nagged at people because I wanted things to
be done well, and efficiency and discipline of work to be
maintained, only I have not always had the right approach,
although my intentions were good – I don't like to harm
anybody and I always saw to it that everybody who deserved
it received a bonus, but on the other hand I severely
punished every unjustified absence, and tried to suppress
slackness and non-fulfilment of quotas, and gave an example
myself how to work. I never counted my own overtime, so
I didn't take into account the others' overtime, this is why
there was some discontent and even protests, but I never
took any notice of the grievances of individuals who did not
understand the socialist approach to work, because they
hindered the fulfilment and exceeding of norms.

My honesty made me lose my health because when I
destroyed the development plans for the Cane-Panel and
Pre-Fabricated One-Family House factory at Wilkasy in
the presence of my brother-in-law, Citizen Victor Tomaszewski . . .

This business with the development plans occurred as
I have already shortly described in my Appeal sent to the
Citizen First Secretary of the Central Committee of the

THE APPEAL

Polish United Workers' Party, Warsaw. I was greatly distressed that my activities in a managerial post had been so tendentiously and unjustly interpreted, and I took these documents from my desk in the presence of my brother-in-law, Citizen Victor Tomaszewski, employed in the aforementioned factory as a mycologist, and this same Victor Tomaszewski subsequently turned into a Judas for me, but at the time he had not yet sold himself to my persecutors, and even asked me: 'What are these papers, Marian?' 'Papers,' I answered and added: 'Let's go, I'll never darken the doors of this place again.' We both went to the side wing, where I had the use of a small room to spend the night in on the occasions when I did overtime late into the night. I put the folder with the plans on the table. 'Calm yourself, Marian,' said my brother-in-law, 'you get unnecessarily excited, try to look at everything coolly, you must admit that people are not entirely wrong.' 'You are against me too,' I said bitterly, for I saw clearly that I had been manoeuvred into a losing position. 'I am not against you,' he said, probably in order to comfort me, 'because I know how well you have worked and how much you have done to further the development of the factory.' 'That is probably why you are against me,' I said. 'Don't get excited,' he said again, 'I'm telling you that I am not against you, but you must admit, people can't have been pleased when a list of shortcomings and wrongdoings was read out to them in public.' 'Was it untrue?' I exclaimed, 'It was true,' he admitted, 'but it was not pleasant.' Then I said: 'I'm sorry, Victor, but it isn't my job to gloss over reality and I shall never say that white is black or black is white, you cannot expect me to do so because I am not prompted

65

by any private interest.' 'I know, Marian,' he said, 'and I don't want you to gloss over reality.' 'Well then?' I asked. 'New times are coming, Marian,' he said, 'a thaw, and your behaviour might be interpreted as harking back to the period of mistakes and misinterpretations and continuing the cult of the individual, wait, let me finish – what could people have thought when they learned that you kept personal files on them and entered everything they did during working hours and after work, and even, if you'll excuse me, in their own beds? Many people thought you acted like a martinet and wanted to decide everything in the factory by yourself, and that you disregarded collective decisions – they were right to think this, and if they did it was largely your own fault, Marian. Your tactics were wrong, now you have to bear the consequences.'

I was so angry that I had to take a strong hold of myself not to blow my top, but I repeated calmly: 'My tactics were wrong, you say; so perhaps Baranski did not sell factory materials on the side, Urbaniak did not come drunk to work, Rybkowski did not maltreat his wife and children, Nowak did not put a number of girls in the family way and refuse to pay up, Wachowiak did not listen every evening to Free Europe broadcasts, Malachowski did not take bribes, Wolny did not have the money to wear new clothes all the time, smoke the best cigarettes and pay a yard-long bill in the Albatross every Saturday? And as for Eddie Zuch, how many times did he get into trouble with the Militia for disorderly behaviour when drunk – and it wasn't his doing that he didn't get dragged to court, was it? And Roleczek had contacts with suspect individuals from the private sector of industry, and Sroka told anti-Soviet jokes and spread defeatist rumours against the Party and the Government.'

I might have gone on for a long time, enumerating the various larger or smaller trespasses of my collaborators, but Victor interrupted me. 'All this is true, Marian, I know it is, but if it is true, you should have taken action immediately, and not stored it all away in one big bag.' 'Just think, Victor,' I said, 'you are talking like an ignorant, unenlightened peasant, if I had really done anything about what wasn't in order, who would have been left to do the work, I ask you? I would have had to sack three-quarters of my personnel, without any notice, as a disciplinary measure. Don't be childish, Victor, I collected information in order to know what was going on in my factory and to know who I was dealing with – to be able to say to them, if I ever wanted to speak in confidence to any of them: Listen you, Nowak, or Malachowski, don't tell me any lies, because nothing escapes my notice, I know everything about you, but I don't wish you any harm, I have trust in you as a positive member of the community and only demand that you should stop doing so-and-so, or alter your way of life a bit and not bring disrepute to your factory by your behaviour. Just tell me, was I wrong? This was a long-term intention, it's easy to fire a man, more difficult to educate him.' 'Perhaps you were right,' replied my brother-in-law, 'only the results were not what you had intended.' 'Not what I had intended?' I repeated after him and felt a terrible pressure in my breast. 'Time will show,' I said, 'if others will act as they should when I am gone.'

Then, I remember, I opened the folder which lay on the desk and, not hurrying at all, very calmly, I began to tear up those plans. 'Come to your senses, Marian!' exclaimed

Victor, 'what are these papers?' 'Just papers,' I answered
and pushed him away, because he wanted to stop me, but I
was determined, 'these development plans were my own
idea, drawn up on my own initiative, so if I am evil and
a public enemy, they can be destroyed too,' and I continued
to tear them up and throw the bits into a waste-paper
basket. Later I threw them in the fire, and as the embers
were hot they burned very quickly. I saw Victor grow pale
and wipe his forehead. 'Marian,' he said, 'do you know
what will happen now?' 'There will be some smoke,' I
answered, 'open the window, there's a smell of burning.'
'Marian,' he said, 'there is a smell, I know, but a smell of
the public prosecutor.' 'Don't try to frighten me,' I said,
'I am as pure as the driven snow.'

Only later did I understand what misfortune I brought
upon my head by destroying those plans. 'It is your own
fault that people are talking – if you had not provided
reasons, they would not have had any ammunition against
you,' I heard these words said to me a hundred times and
more by my wife and in-laws, I was so fed up with this that
I stopped reacting to their talk, because I have always
known that even if I had not torn up and burned those
development plans for the factory at Wilkasy, my enemies
would have found another weak point in my activities,
because if you want to strike somebody as if he is a drum,
you will always find a way of striking – but the point is I
am not a drum, I am a living human being who has lost his
health through being honest, because as soon as I had torn
up and burned those plans in the presence of my brother-in-
law, Citizen Victor Tomaszewski, I immediately went to my
technical deputy, Engineer Casimir Borsuk, and told him

what had happened, and he was a decent man and explained at once that nothing had happened, that he had a copy of the plans, but being honest I told the whole truth to the Personnel Officer, I might have kept it quiet, but did not do so, acting in the best of faith and not thinking that by so doing I was exposing myself to gossip and slander, which was in accordance with the intentions of my enemies, so that I should drift to a crisis. Although for eight years I had not been aware of any enemy action, being blind and deaf, things were not right around me, I felt that not everything was as it should be, but I didn't notice the essence of the problem. When I was working at the State Co-operative of Food Producers at Lidzbark, I felt that people were acting strangely towards me, shutting up when I unexpectedly entered a room, but I pretended not to notice anything, although my isolation kept increasing. I have always been sociable and frank, I have never liked to walk alone, always been open with people, I used to suggest to various colleagues to come with me for a beer, but it always happened that each of them excused himself with various duties and so I'd end up having my beer alone.

Once, I remember, I happened to invite my colleague Casimir Dominik of the Planning Department to a bar for a beer and he excused himself saying that he had to meet his wife, and an hour later I met him there having a drink with a large, exclusively male group – if there had been any women present I would have understood, but no, Mr Dominik was drinking with a group of men and he even pretended not to see me, he pointedly turned his back on me, although he was both younger and in a more junior position – I couldn't stand it and after one large vodka and

one large beer I walked up to his table and said not too
loudly but not too softly either: 'Hi, Dominik, I see that
you must have missed your lady!' Only then did he turn
round towards me, but was not embarrassed at all, laughed
in my face and asked: 'Why? Have you got anything to say
to my wife? I could take a message.' So this is what you
are like! I thought to myself and said: 'There is no message, because I have nothing to say to your wife, only I could
not help noticing that you have changed your plans,
Dominik.' Then, quite brazenly, he said: 'And what did you
imagine, Mr Konieczny – that I was a cow?' Taken aback
I asked: 'Why a cow?' to which he said: 'Because it is
only a cow that chews the cud and shits, but never changes
its habits and views, while I am a free citizen and do as I
please, and what's more I don't like it at all when strangers
interfere in my private affairs and boorishly accost me.
Have I expressed myself clearly, Mr Konieczny?' I shook
with indignation at his abuse and being unable to contain
myself said: 'It's boors like me, Mr Dominik, who fought
for Poland against the Nazi invaders and shed their blood
when you were running around in short pants and peeing in
them.' This is what I said and turned away, but I could
hear how they all burst out laughing offensively. I had to
take a grip on myself to return to my table, and when I
sat down I felt my hands shaking, so I ordered another
vodka and a small beer; Miss Yola, the waitress, looked at
me strangely, but served it; I tried all the while not to look
towards the others, but when I had gulped down my vodka
I looked all the same and what did I see? Mr Dominik was
doing the same thing. I had a most disagreeable feeling so I
lifted my glass of beer, and he did the very same although,

I could swear, he did not seem to be looking at me, he was turning his back on me as he had done before I spoke to him. I waited for a moment and then, not moving my eyes from Dominik, I lifted my left hand and stroked my hair with my palm – I felt a sudden shiver in my bones because Dominik made the same gesture. I was almost certain that by doing this he wanted to signal something to me, only I didn't know what, so I waited another moment, finished my beer, and then reached into the pocket of my trousers for my handkerchief. I looked again stealthily – he too was holding a handkerchief in his hand, only he produced it from his top jacket pocket, not from his trousers: now I shall check on you, I thought, and as my forehead was wet with perspiration, I wiped it with my handkerchief and was naïve enough to think he would do the same, but he wiped his nose instead and folded his handkerchief and put it back in his jacket pocket. I felt terrible at that moment, as if the earth had shaken under me, because for the first time I realized that I was being watched and that my enemies had gone so far in their persecution that they chose to let me know that they were vigilant and watching every step I took. This happened on 4th March 1963 and only the next day did I realize that it was Casimir Dominik's nameday, he must have entertained his friends with his traitor's daily pay – later, I believe, he was receiving an ordinary spy's salary.

Since serving with the Citizens' Militia I had avoided heavy drinking, I occasionally had a glass, perhaps two in company, but never by myself, but that evening after I had left the bar – and it can't have been later than seven pm – I went the rounds, as the saying goes, and I can't remember how and when I returned home, my head ached terribly the next day and I couldn't quench my thirst at home, so on the way to work I bought myself a small lager in a kiosk, and as I was carrying a brief-case I stood it on the pavement against the kiosk and had begun to drink the beer when I felt as if struck by a thunderbolt. On the other side of the counter an unknown man had also stood his case on the pavement and begun to drink a small lager, looking strangely at me while doing so, so I looked at my watch, he did the same, I lit a cigarette, a Sport, he did the same, but his was Extra Strong. What now? I thought to myself, not every spy can smoke Sports, and no sooner did I think that, than the other man leant down and asked for a packet of Sports. All this happened in March 1963, that is a whole year earlier than the date I caught my brother-in-law spying on me. I suppose it all had a higher purpose – to confuse, worry and crush me so that I should be forced to reveal the password, which was the key to my alleged spying – they had never clearly said that, they were too sly to uncover all their trumps, but from the moment I stopped being blind and deaf, I knew full well what their object was and what they were aiming for, damn them!

And now I shall report the conversation which I had with Citizen Richard Kuna, Chairman of the State Co-operative of Food Producers at Lidzbark, my old pal from the Citizens' Militia whom I met after I had left preventive arrest at Swiatki and thanks to whom I was appointed Deputy Manager of the butcher's shop at Lidzbark. I feel it my duty to mention that conversation, because it is an important link in the chain which was being forged for fettering and strangling me, but why me, a grey ordinary citizen, an insignificant pawn, I still don't know – why it was me who was selected as a victim? I sometimes think it was nobody's fault or ill will, only hard necessity, for every machine, in order to function efficiently, must be fed, otherwise it will start stalling and working badly, but perhaps I am wrong and everything has quite a different purpose. Everything is too confusing, it is better not to ponder over what, how and why, human understanding is too feeble, one must hold on to one's national and social reason and not let up when hostile elements from the Counter-intelligence start to hound one.

I first made a report on the above-mentioned conversation with Citizen Richard Kuna in 1963, when I had it fresh in my memory, at the suggestion of Citizen Registrar Dr Stefan Plebanski for his personal perusal, because he had asked me to write down certain episodes of my life, which I did. I always carry copies of these documents on me so that no outsider should see them, I still keep them in a separate folder. So that Citizen First Secretary may be completely informed I shall copy that document, not changing anything in it because everything was truthfully recorded. I must add only that the conversation took place in April 1963 and that the incident upset me a lot, but soon I was to experience with my own skin that the hostile hand would set even worse snares for me. As to that conversation, I must mention that on that day, going to work, I drank a large lager in the kiosk in 22nd July Street, but no one was watching me then, or else I didn't notice anything, I didn't feel well, I had drunk a little the previous day, but not too much, only enough to drown my sorrow, I felt rather ill, altogether I was becoming increasingly restless and given to outbursts of temper, or I'd fall into a torpor – called traumatic anaesthesia – and have no wish to do anything, no desire to live, but there were objective reasons for my condition, anybody else in my place would have felt even worse.

I feel obliged to confirm that Citizen Registrar Dr Plebanski has more than once, and always in a friendly manner, explained to me that my illness consists of a delusion, namely that, because of my neurotic state, I am only imagining that the Counter-intelligence is persecuting me, that no one accuses me of high treason and considers me an agent of foreign intelligence, and this apparently has been checked with the provincial Security Office. I well understand Dr Plebanski's point of view, because it is motivated by the noblest of intentions, he wishes to lift up my spirits and comfort me, so I won't have any discussions on that subject, moreover the Registrar knows my uncompromising attitude to the matter and I assume he respects it and appreciates that I am not an opportunist and that at the cost of my health and my nerves I have become engaged in a fight for true justice.

I promise myself a good deal from the appeal I sent out, it will take some time before I get an answer, but I must prepare myself now for the eventuality of being invited to a personal audience with the Citizen First Secretary of the Central Committee, so I must work very efficiently in order to be ready to take a trip to Warsaw and, just in case, I must have the full documentation, all the details in my case are of prime importance and I am convinced that after getting acquainted with my appeal the Citizen First Secretary will wish to see me and ask for a full dossier.

THE APPEAL

My persecutors deny all their machinations, they have always responded in this way to questioning by third parties and this is how I explain the fact of Citizen Registrar Dr Plebanski's faulty assessment, they must have extraordinarily sure methods to be able to get round even such an educated and enlightened person as the Registrar, but I believe that faced with the authority of Citizen First Secretary their hypocritical excuses and tendentious falsifications of facts will be exposed and they will have to capitulate. In Jugoslavia last summer their Minister of Security tried to dominate the Party and the Government, but he was unmasked in time and relieved of all his offices and dignities, and that's a warning to all those who try to dominate the Party and join the ranks of the enemy. Citizen First Secretary is certainly insufficiently informed in many instances, perhaps even consciously misinformed, from this point of view therefore my petition, though coming from an ordinary citizen, might be a salutary alarm signal, because the wrong done to me is not the private affair of one individual but a far wider issue, only it must be presented properly, and I am sure that this is what the leadership of the Party will do and I regret that only now . . .

I forgot to mention an important thing: today, to be precise this morning, that sociologist arrived in the clinic, as the Registrar had announced, he came with his wife, she is apparently also a sociologist and works at the University, she seemed to me a very handsome woman, he is a fine figure too, tall, well built and fair, I would say he looks like a sportsman or an actor, not like a scholar and rather young, I wouldn't have thought him more than thirty, but from Sister Irena who received him in the treatment room I learned that he is thirty-six, his Christian name is Matthew, I have forgotten his surname, something short – he doesn't look a sick man, he's very sunburnt, probably spent his holiday somewhere on a lake or went on an Orbis tour to the south, he has his own pyjamas and dressing-gown, you can see at once it's of foreign make; his eyes are rather restless, and altogether he is a little bit over-animated, I am curious what his trouble is, it doesn't look like depression or an anxiety state, perhaps alcohol or some other drug? For the time being he has been allotted the bed in the corridor, vacated by the doctor who committed suicide, but I am sure they will transfer him soon, it is quite possible that he will come to us, to Ward 30, because I don't think the Frenchman will return – he went home yesterday on a pass, but I doubt if he will come back tomorrow morning, I don't think he will, instead he'll send his wife to collect his things, he won't appear again himself, this is what he hinted to us before leaving. I am astonished that they gave him a pass at all, because yesterday there was a great row with the Registrar: during Dr Plebanski's rounds the Frenchman began to talk big and even said that he was quite well, and the Registrar got terribly angry, and started shouting that only he can decide who is and who is not well, and that one word from him would suffice for an undisciplined patient to be transported to Tworki or Drewnica.

Raphael is all right, I must have imagined things at the time, he's a very decent boy, I am very fond of him, he's quite bright, he has even learned to play bridge a little, although when he came here he couldn't tell one suit from another and didn't know the court cards. I don't know when the sociologist will begin work in the psychologist's room, for the moment he doesn't look capable of concentrating on an abstract subject, but just in case, I am mentally preparing myself to come here tomorrow, but from Monday on to work in the ward, so that there shouldn't be any conflicts, and this is what I reported to the Registrar this morning, but he didn't say anything, just heard me out, but I believe . . . I must finish now because I am beginning to feel increasingly restless and my hand is turning dead.

*

On Monday morning, at eleven am when the Colonel and Raphael had gone for a walk, Konieczny put their absence to good use. Unfolding the exercise book on his bed he noted:

I forgot to add yesterday the text of the conversation which I had with Citizen Richard Kuna, Director of the State Co-operative of Food Producers at Lidzbark and my former colleague in the Citizens' Militia at Augustow, prepared in accordance with the previous record of that conversation in the summer of 1963 at the request of Citizen Registrar Dr Stefan Plebanski. As I have a copy of this record with me I can faithfully inform the Citizen First Secretary about it. I must mention that the conversation took place in Citizen Richard Kuna's office where he summoned me as soon as I arrived at work. I have always been careful to address Citizen Richard Kuna in public in an official manner, and I only addressed him in the familiar form when we were alone face to face.

Cit. Kuna: How are you, old man! Why are you so pale? – admit it, you've had a merry‑night, old cock!

I: What an idea, I couldn't care less for things like that.

Cit. Kuna: A pity, it would do your nerves a lot of good.

I: I am quite all right. I don't need such medicines.

Cit. Kuna: I can see, Marian, that you don't wish to be frank with me. You see, old man, I don't keep a check on my staff as you once used to at Wilkasy, but none the less I am quite well informed about what is going on in this office and elsewhere. What is it that makes you get in people's hair all the time? Why is the place humming with gossip about you?

I: I don't do anything.

Cit. Kuna: This is bad. You know, Marian, how many telephone calls I get about your behaviour, and anonymous letters? Take this morning. I got three saying that Citizen Konieczny said so-and-so, Citizen Konieczny is such-and-such.

I: And do you believe them?

Cit. Kuna: Don't get excited, Marian. Who said anything about my believing them? I have known you for some time, I know you're a decent fellow, but you must try to understand my position: when people complain about one of my colleagues, I have to do something about it. What did you say to Dominik the day before yesterday? Try to remember.

I: I can remember quite well what I said to Citizen Dominik.

Cit. Kuna: That he was spying on you and was an agent of some Counter-intelligence?

I: He is not the only one.

Cit. Kuna: Am I perhaps one as well?

I: For the moment I have nothing against you, Richard.

Cit. Kuna: For the moment, you said? Well, from an old pal I've helped when he was in a sticky situation – that's something. . . . Listen, Marian, I'll be frank with you, I don't wish to be anything else. Wouldn't you like to see a good doctor? I'm serious. I hear there's a clinic for nervous diseases in town –

I: Are you saying I am a lunatic?

Cit. Kuna: On the contrary, I'm advising you to have treatment so that you don't become one, can't you understand? There's nothing to be ashamed of, times are not easy, and not everybody has nerves as strong as our frontier on the Oder-Neisse, think about it, we'll help you, give you sick leave, you'll get treatment, have a rest, calm your nerves – medical science has made a lot of progress lately, I assure you this is good advice.

I: Citizen Dominik is probably with you in this?

Cit. Kuna: Why have you got your knife in him? He said you were looking for a quarrel.

I: Then why is he spying on me and aping me?

Cit. Kuna: Aping you? Marian!

I:	Well, the day before yesterday I went to the bar for a beer, and he aped everything I did, he imitated every single thing.
Cit. Kuna:	Oh, Marian, Marian, old chap, things are much worse with you than I thought. Just think quietly for a moment, why should Dominik want to ape you?
I:	He knows very well why. And what do you think, where did he get the money from to buy himself a Lambretta for thirty thousand last week?
Cit. Kuna:	What do you mean? Didn't you know he won money on the pools? He had five draws.
I:	It may be true he did have five – but not from the pools, I know those pools. If you want to know I'll tell you. It's by spying on me that Citizen Dominik got enough money to lord it and ride around all over the town, the damn' Judas!

I have no further record of my conversation with Citizen Kuna, because towards the end of it I became very agitated, but what I have quoted above is sufficient proof of the intrigues that were spun around me and how in that situation even a supposed friend like Citizen Kuna adopted an opportunist attitude – he himself may not have been directly connected with the Counter-intelligence, but once he realized how things were, he preferred not to stick his neck out and washed his hands of it all like Pontius Pilate, which hurt me very much and depressed me, because he must have been ungrateful enough to have forgotten the years of our common soldierly hardships, when a man waking up in the morning had no certainty that he would live to see the evening and not be killed by a treacherous enemy bullet. I have now forgiven Citizen Kuna for having adopted such an opportunist attitude towards me, because he is dead and if one is to sum him up, he was a decent man, he only became too fond of his comforts and stopped being a fighter, but Our Gracious Lord, after weighing up his virtues and his sins, probably didn't judge him too severely and didn't send him to eternal damnation, the sociologist didn't go out for a walk but walked up and down the corridor, when he passed I noticed he looked several times in my direction.

*

That afternoon, in the psychologist's room

INFORMATION NOTE
To the Citizen First Secretary
of the Central Committee of the
Polish United Workers' Party
and to the Leadership of the
Party
RE:
breaches of legality committed
by elements of the Counter-intelligence

When snooping on me and trying to provoke me, various methods have been applied against my person, including the use of the Electronic Brain, which I can merely mention because my knowledge is insufficient to report in detail how the aforementioned Brain functions and in what way its spying activities manifest themselves. But I am in a position to state most emphatically that the Electronic Brain has been used for special missions, namely when agents and spies proved to be inadequate and when it was necessary to find out what I was up to when alone. I am in possession of numerous proofs that at various times situations of an intimate character were purposely brought about, and this was done so skilfully and discreetly that only I myself could understand the meaning of certain gestures and grimaces suggested by the agents. I trust that the Leadership of the Party will take appropriate steps to establish all the circumstances connected with the activities of the Electronic Brain, because it is possible that this kind of powerful and dangerous weapon in the hands of irresponsible elements might also be used against the Leadership, to undermine the unity of the Party or against the democratic foundations of Socialist building.

Apart from the Electronic Brain, the action of the Counter-intelligence against my person has principally been apparent in: (1) organizing a net of agents and spies, watching over all my activities (2) training those agents and spies to keep me, by incessant aping, under constant nervous tension, a very tiring thing, and (3) using as stooges persons known to me personally or by sight, in order to establish if I would recognize them as agents of a foreign intelligence service and betray the password to them which I am falsely accused of possessing.

I

It is difficult for me to state precisely how many agents

and spies the Counter-intelligence has sent out to watch and spy on me, but I estimate that there were approximately thirty thousand persons of both sexes. In saying this I base myself on real facts, namely that, although I have a good visual memory, I have never observed, in the space of twelve years, the same man or woman appearing twice within my field of vision as a snooper, I assume therefore that for controlling every step I took, including travel to work and journeys to the Technical College at Lodz as well as to T for medical purposes, at least seven agents daily had to be used, one set of three and two pairs, which gives us a monthly figure of 210 hirelings, yearly 2,520, and over twelve years 30,240. I take into account that the above figure only approximately represents the scope of the action mounted against me as it does not take into account those like my brother-in-law, Citizen Victor Tomaszewski, or others in the places of work where I have been employed who were on permanent agent's pay for as long as objective circumstances demanded it. I am unable to establish even approximately how many persons of both sexes were in the latter category, certainly quite a large number, and all this must have cost enormous sums of money, not to mention costs of a moral nature which must have been very high too.

Contrary to permanent agents on the payroll, recruited for certain functions to be performed and acting individually, the mass of agents put on to me rarely act singly, and for tactical reasons are usually organized in pairs or threes, in order to give their selected victim a general idea of the powerful means at the disposal of the Counter-intelligence. Observation of a person, I have noticed, never lasts a whole

day, because efficient organization means continuous passing on of information, so that those sent out in pairs or
threes can limit themselves to occasional appearances, but
behave in such a manner that the person watched is incessantly convinced that he is being trailed and controlled. I
believe that the organizational system of the Counter-
intelligence, which undoubtedly has something to do with
the Electronic Brain, transferred to a different area and
properly exploited, might bring many benefits in the political, social and economic fields, but this would require a
serious study in depth, also operators who are experienced
and ideologically reliable.

2

The activities of both categories of agents, i.e. those on the
permanent payroll and in the mass, are based first of all on
a repetition of situations in which the person watched finds
himself, or else a repetition of actions, gestures and facial
expressions which he makes – the behaviour of Citizen
Casimir Dominik and my brother-in-law Citizen Victor
Tomaszewski being very typical in this respect.

3

The Counter-intelligence has also in its service a third
category of agents and these receive the highest salaries,
because along with many characteristics necessary for spies,
they must possess very special qualities, for which they
are selected and screened from amongst many thousands
of candidates – the role which they perform is that of

provocateur. I met with this phenomenon for the first time in the autumn of 1963 when His Eminence the Cardinal Primate of Poland came on a visit and, having learned the date and hour of arrival of the Distinguished Guest from one of the priests, I proceeded to the church of St Peter and Paul and along with many others of the Faithful took part in the welcome to the Prince of the Church, shouting with the others: 'Long live the Cardinal!' Three weeks later when one afternoon I went into a restaurant to have a beer, I was faced with the Cardinal or rather with his double, a provocateur. At first I didn't notice him, only when I sat down and looked around the place, I saw him sitting alone at a table under the window, of course in civilian clothes, in a dark suit – he was eating a pork chop, and drinking beer with it. At first I could have sworn that this was the Cardinal himself, they must have looked a long time to find such an identical double, I at once understood that they had thought I would never suspect that deceit, that I would establish contact and, who knows, perhaps even reveal the password, but they don't know enough about the customs of the Princes of the Church, because if they had been knowledgeable about such delicate matters, they would not have given false instructions to the double, as it was, through oversight or ignorance, the false Cardinal kept looking towards me all the time so insistently that I guessed at once I was dealing with an impostor and a provocateur, and I got up without finishing my beer, paid and left the restaurant.

This was the first time they faced me with an authentic personality, later on many occasions similar actions took place and as the persons confronting me were not so highly placed as the Cardinal, I could not always discover the deceit at once. Once for example in September 1966, I met by chance in the street a man who had served with me at Augustow in the Citizens' Militia, but at the end of 1945 was unmasked as a member of the National Armed Forces and later sentenced to twenty-five years' imprisonment, only it turned out that because of the Amnesty to mark Poland's Thousandth Anniversary he was discharged earlier, we did not talk for very long, because after so many years and such drastic experiences we had little to say to each other, he was only in town in transit and had to catch a train to Gdansk in the evening, so we parted.

The next day, when I went out shopping in the morning, I saw him near the newspaper kiosk, he was walking up and down as if he was waiting for somebody, so not wanting him to believe that I didn't wish to have anything to do with him because of his past, I went up to him and said: 'You didn't go to Gdansk, I see.' He looked at me rather strangely and said: 'Give me a hundred zloty and I'll go.' I was slightly taken aback, but not much, for I thought at once that he must be short of money for the ticket and as I had some money on me to do the shopping I produced a hundred-zloty note and said: 'I can't give you a hundred, because I won't have enough for shopping, but I can lend you fifty.' 'Let's have fifty,' he said, 'let's have the note, I'll change it.' I gave him the note, he took it and went up to the newspaper kiosk, returned with the two fifties, gave me one, put the other in his pocket and said: 'You could stand me a drink now, Wacek.' 'I don't drink,' I said, for after my stay in the clinic, on Registrar Dr Plebanski's advice, I have never taken alcohol, only occasionally a small beer when the weather is very hot, and I added: 'My name is Marian, not Wacek.' 'Never mind,' he said, 'Marian is good enough to stand me a drink,' and he smiled so crookedly while saying it that I could see his toothless mouth. I at once understood the situation, which was that he was not the real Wladek Jesionowski, because Wladek, although he had spent so many years in gaol, has kept all his teeth, white as a wolf's so that when that provocateur spoke to me so cheekily I quickly left him, I didn't even ask him for the return of the fifty zloty for I was pleased not to have got involved in worse trouble unwittingly if I had gone for a drink with him.

This is how that unpleasant incident ended, but many more people I know have been impersonated in various circumstances, thus for instance, I have been confronted with doubles of Citizen Franciszek Wachowiak, my former colleague in the Cane-Panel and Pre-Fabricated One-Family House factory at Wilkasy, Citizen Dr Zofia Mlodzianowska of the Psychosomatic Clinic at T who held conversations with me on the Registrar's instructions in 1963 and 1964, also Citizen Maria Bratek, who underwent treatment at the clinic because of an anxiety state accompanied by paralysis of the legs so that she couldn't walk, I occasionally helped her and on these occasions talked to her a lot about life and other general subjects. Always however I guessed the identity of the impersonator in time and unmasked the provocations of my enemies, which saved me from more serious complications and other dangers.

And now I must finish, because it is half past nine, this is my last moment in the psychologist's room and I can't find words to express my gratitude to these four walls which have stood guard over my work for all the last seven days. I have come to feel quite at home in this place and now when the time has come to leave it I feel as if I have left a part of myself here inside these walls, but dead walls are better than people because they don't eavesdrop and have no power of speech. Farewell, my dear walls!

*

In the course of Monday Konieczny wrote, in his room and in the corridor:

My diagnosis of the Frenchman's intentions has proved to be quite correct because as I had foreseen he did not return to the clinic last night, today he did not show up either, but his wife came instead – she didn't stay long in the Registrar's office and as I was in the corridor I saw her leave, very agitated. Later Sister Irena helped her to collect her husband's personal belongings while I tactfully remained in the corridor. He didn't act properly, a grown-up and educated man should not behave like this, I am astonished at such behaviour, I never felt much sympathy for him but I would have preferred him to act like a man, this is not a good advertisement for his industrious and talented nation . . .

We usually play bridge in the same company, myself, the Colonel and the two engineers Skowronski who had never met before and only discovered here that their families both come from the same village in the province of Kielce – and by a further chance they are both civil engineers, except that Zbigniew Skowronski lives at Szczecin, and the other, Bronislav, in Warsaw, both used to suffer from depressions but now they are much better. We play quite a good game in this four, but today the Colonel didn't want to play after dinner because he felt a cold coming on, he wanted to lie down, so we looked for a fourth and it turned out that Dr Matthew Gwara likes bridge. We invited him, he is a very nice man and plays quite well, only he likes to use the club convention which we don't know very well, so we played normally, he is a pleasant player, a little uneven perhaps as he gets carried away. At one point, when he and I were partners, after I bid two spades he at once auctioned a small slam in spades, I was two down, although I might have made my bid but my nerve failed me and I didn't bid the clubs on the table properly, he was not angry at all and even looked as pleased as if we had had a grand slam instead of a small one, later, after we had played three rubbers, he pulled me aside and said he had been told by the Registrar that I had been using the psychologist's room, and he said if my work required it I could continue to use it, because for the moment he couldn't think of doing any serious work, perhaps in a few days' time he will after he has become acclimatized to the new surroundings and conditions.

Later he asked me in a most friendly manner what my occupation was and I was pleased that, although he is so highly educated, he listened to me with attention and understanding and so, one thing leading to another, I told him a lot about myself. We were walking up and down the corridor because I can talk best when walking, I don't get so agitated when I am moving about, but he was obviously not used to walking in such a confined space and began to look round for a seat and listened with less attention, until at last he said: 'Don't be cross, Mr. Konieczny, but I don't like walking up and down, it reminds me of prison.' I could not stop myself and said: 'But, surely, Doctor, you have not been in prison?' And he said: 'Is that what you think? Then you are wrong, for one Pole in every three has been in prison for one thing or another, and I am the third.' 'A man like you,' I said, 'it's hard to believe, but if you have really earned a prison sentence it must have been for being a patriot, that's what I think.' He burst out laughing but didn't say anything more, he didn't confirm or deny my words, so I didn't insist, only thought to myself that if a man like Dr Gwara has been in prison I should feel better in my misfortune, but I didn't feel any relief, on the contrary my heart felt heavy, but as we were sitting down at the table in the corridor I said: 'Excuse me, Doctor, I feel rather restless now,' and explained to him about this restlessness, that it is a side effect of an anxiety state and will pass entirely when I return home and start up a normal marital relationship with my wife again. At this moment the woman in the pink dressing-gown appeared as if from out of the ground and said to me: 'Oh, so Mr Konieczny is not writing today!' I felt rather embarrassed at this impertinent remark, but calmly tried to counter it. 'And how do you know that I write?' I said. She laughed cheekily: 'Is it a secret?' she asked. 'No, it isn't a secret,' I replied, 'only I myself never ask you what you are doing.' She again laughed: 'You may ask me anything you like,' she said, 'I have no secrets from you.' 'Even if you had any secrets,' I replied, 'I am not inquisitive.' 'Oh, what an unkind man you are!' she said, 'I speak to you in a friendly fashion, and you at once get

offended.' 'I don't get offended,' I said with emphasis,
'but I don't like . . .' I didn't finish what I wanted to say,
because Dr Gwara interrupted the conversation, I can't
remember what he said, something rather intelligent,
because the Pink Woman at once calmed down, said something and walked away.

We didn't revert to our unfinished conversation, because
my restlessness increased owing to that incident, so I apolo-
gized to Dr Gwara and went to my room, but although I
was almost alone, because the Colonel was asleep and
Raphael was playing draughts in the women's section, I
couldn't work, because my hand kept slipping away, so I
lay down but couldn't fall asleep, I had too many thoughts,
until I came to the conclusion that in view of the latest
development I must take great care and be specially on my
guard.

She came to the clinic from Internal Diseases a week
or so ago, a blonde, looks twenty-five or -six, she wears a
pink robe and a nightgown which is also pink, but much
lighter, I don't know what her trouble is, but she is very
agitated, has flushed cheeks and suspiciously brilliant eyes,
she is always in and out of the men's section, she has looked
into our ward several times and tried to establish contact
with the Frenchman and the Colonel – until now she has
avoided me, so I was taken aback when she spoke to me
directly today. Lately I've noticed that she has calmed
down, she has begun to play nurses and is forever pushing
the invalid chair of a young boy who was brought in last
Wednesday night after a tram accident with his leg in
plaster, he must have suffered from shock, because he
groaned all through the night and had nightmares, and the

next day too – he seems better now, but won't speak to anyone, only allows her to push him everywhere, to the lavatory or the bathroom, or just along the corridors, she addresses him as Witold, he calls her 'Monica', the role of nurse probably suits her because it provides a cover and pushing the boy's invalid chair she can move around freely and snoop. God only knows if she has been sent here, I am not one hundred per cent sure, but anyway I must be even more on my guard, a woman like that, if she is well paid, can do more harm than ten men, you don't know when or how and lo and behold! you are caught and dissected like a guinea-pig.

After thinking about it I decided not to use the psychologist's room any more so as not to be exposed to various comments and unnecessary gossip, and also just in case, because I can't be certain whether the Counter-intelligence has got wind about what is going on and taken appropriate steps against me, I know Dr Gwara too little to consult him in this respect, but he too surprised me at one point, namely when he asked me if I would consider my case as definitely cleared and closed if the answer of Citizen First Secretary should state that no one has ever persecuted me and that no accusations of activities inimical to the State have been made against me. At first, I did not quite understand what he meant. 'How can this be possible?' I asked. 'Why,' he said, 'you should take such an answer into account.' To which I replied: 'No, Doctor, I cannot even consider such an eventuality, for it would mean that even the Citizen First Secretary has no access to the truth, and as a loyal citizen I cannot even think of a tragedy of that sort, because in so thinking I would show my lack of faith in the regime, and if I adopted such an attitude I would not be seeking justice from the highest authorities.' I must have convinced Dr Gwara that I was right because he changed the subject and said that he was tired of walking. Afterwards the discussion followed which was interrupted by the Pink Woman, now I am writing in the ward, I have placed the exercise book on the edge of my bed and not even shut the door so as not to awaken suspicions – they may think I am writing a letter home. I am tired and very restless again and my hand is turning dead. I forgot to mention what struck me at once, namely that the Pink Woman looks at men as if she were licking them, I have heard that very many women of that sort work for the Counter-intelligence, not only to spy on foreigners but also on their own fellow-countrymen.

*

On Monday night Konieczny again spoke to Dr Gwara after supper and before the doctors' round. They walked up and down the corridor for a long time. Konieczny did the talking, while the sociologist listened attentively, from time to time skilfully regulating the none too swift current of his companion's confessions by short questions. As he was much taller than Konieczny the sociologist stooped towards him, walking at the side of the short and already paunchy man, markedly adapting his long steps to his shorter ones, his very stance expressing concentration on his companion, he looked like a very young student, carefully making mental notes of the more important points made by an eminent professor; he even quite boyishly knitted his smooth and sunburnt brow. The restlessness and even

93

over-excitement noticed by Konieczny the day before seemed to have disappeared, and at certain moments the flash of special interest, even sympathy or tenderness, could be seen in his keen, sportsman's eyes.

Konieczny did not make a note of the conversation in his exercise book, probably because the accident which took place in the small hours of the morning completely absorbed his attention.

*

In the small hours of Tuesday Konieczny noted:

I was awakened during the night by a terrible scream – we all woke up, because we sleep with the top part of the window open – it was still dark but when I sat up in my bed and pulled the curtain, I saw that it was dawn. We at once guessed that something must have happened in the women's section, because the terrible screaming came from that direction. I remember when I served in the Militia a young girl, the courier for a Nationalist gang, had screamed like this once in the autumn of 1946, at the post, but Corporal Kuna pushed a rag we used to clean shoes with into her mouth, so she stopped – that scream that woke us up was even louder, it was terrible to listen to, I saw by my watch that it was twelve minutes past five, but even when everything quietened down we couldn't sleep. From the ward nurse who came to wash the floor we learned that the girl in the pink robe, Monica, had slipped away from the ward, broken a window in the corridor and been about to jump from it when she was caught just in time, she is apparently terribly cut by the glass, they took her to the surgical ward at once and it isn't certain if she will ever return here. I was very shaken by this event and in view of such a misfortune I began to think that perhaps I had been wrong and suspected the girl unjustly, or maybe it was her conscience that pushed her to this desperate step, the feeling of guilt that she let herself be recruited for dirty work, maybe she had even acted in good faith at first and understood only later what was going on. Everything is possible, I shall never know the full truth unless she tries to re-establish contact when she has recovered and tells me the truth, but I shan't say a cross word to her, because I really feel no resentment now and I am sure that God will forgive her if she dies, and she will be forgiven at the Last Judgment too.

Tuesday

In the morning, Dr Gwara was transferred to our ward, to the bed vacated by the Frenchman – he is a very pleasant and well-brought-up man, he speaks little about himself and I don't ask him any questions, but I assume that he is here for anti-alcoholic treatment, how many valuable individuals have been undermined by alcohol, even destroyed, alcohol is a dangerous enemy of mankind. We played bridge; five of us taking turns. I won one rubber with seven points, lost the second with twelve, because I felt restless and kept getting bad hands. I was becoming more and more agitated, perhaps because I think too much, but I said to myself that come what may, I must make an effort not to neglect anything and try for my petition to have the desired effect and not be wasted – this is why I cannot get rid of certain thoughts about this accursed world and the hell which a human being has to suffer in his lifetime. If it were not for the children, I would sink into a mood of resignation, I am so tired and it seems to me that things are continuously happening behind my back which I know nothing about, hence my restlessness. I unjustly suspected first Raphael and then that poor girl, although I would not swear that she was completely innocent, there must have been some reason why she wanted to take her own life.

I too had suicidal thoughts at one time when I was surrounded by nothing but agents operating in pairs or threes and watching my every step, even when I took a bus or a train to go to work at Lidzbark, there wasn't a day without two or three of them riding with me, they didn't even conceal themselves, because they must have been given these directives by their superiors, they were openly aping me, I couldn't cough without one of the Guardian Angels doing the same, and when I went out into the corridor other agents immediately came out of other compartments as well, and later at Lidzbark they accompanied me from the station to the State Co-operative of Food Producers, each one passing me on to another – in my place of work I was also surrounded by an enormous number of Judases, I clenched my teeth and tried to do my job, but how can a person work productively under such conditions? Especially as at home I did not have any peace either, because my enemies, not content with having bought over my brother-in-law, Citizen Victor Tomaszewski – I don't know when and by what means – even got through to my wife and turned her so much against me that she changed very much for the worse, began to strike up acquaintance with strange men, keeping it secret from me, stopped caring for the home and for the children. This is how she showed her gratitude for all my work and my devotion to her, trampling on all the goodwill I had for her. Often I used to go mad with worry because I didn't know what to think of her loyalty to me, I felt as alone as a stone in the road, friends had left me, my family had betrayed me, I was surrounded by nothing but enemies and why had it all happened to me? One day I decided to finish it all, to drown myself or throw myself under a train to put an end to my sufferings, but somehow the Lord stopped me from taking this step, I felt however that if things were to continue as they were I would go mad.

On the day which was to have been my last, not saying anything to anybody, not even to my wife, I walked to the station, incessantly watched by agents, waited for the Poznan train, and when I got out at T it was night, so I don't know whether the spies lost track of me, I didn't think about it at the time because I was so terribly tired. Straight from the station I went to my sister Citizen Barbara Konieczna and sought refuge with her, and although we had never been very close and had met only a few times since the war, she received me like a true sister, and seeing the condition I was in took care of me – I couldn't tell her anything or explain anything, for whenever I wanted to open my heart to her I began to weep and thought I would choke with tears. My sister was appalled at my condition and what had become of me and – through contacts she has at the Bishop's Curia where she works – managed to get a place for me at Registrar Dr Stefan Plebanski's clinic, and to my great relief he found room for me. For the first few weeks the enemy persecuted me even there, skilfully choosing various individuals from amongst the patients and staff so that I was under observation all the time and each of my actions was aped, only later, seeing that my condition was improving, they left me alone and postponed further machinations and plots for a time – this is a known method of torture: so as not to finish off the victim too soon they interrupt the torture so that the prisoner can taste it all the better when he has recovered some of his strength.

I was beaten terribly by the Gestapo at Suwalki, especially on the legs, my legs were so swollen that I was unable to walk, I lost consciousness a number of times, they threw water on me, brought me round and left me alone for a time, but as soon as I felt stronger they would start on me again – I was only seventeen at the time, I thought this was my end and that I would perish without having tasted life at the hands of the Fascist tormentors.

I have never been strong, I have always been highly strung, for being a sixth child there was little for me to take from my mother's womb, this is why I am not very tall and why my nerves are weak. When I was released from prison after bribing a member of the Gestapo my father, although he was a tough character, wrung his hands and cried when he saw what they had done with his own flesh and blood, I was the shadow of a man, as if I had come back from the dead, for the three months of investigation I had lived through terrible things and even now I sometimes dream I am being tortured, and in these dreams I am naked and shivering with cold and a horrible fear and although my eyes are closed I can feel two or three Gestapo-men approach me, I can hear their heavy breathing, they come up to me and one standing behind me grabs me by the

throat and pulls my head back and with his other hand
which is heavy and sweaty shuts my mouth so that I cannot scream, while the other two begin to kick me in the
small of my back and in my private parts, then beat me on
the thighs with iron rods. It is a horrible dream, I wake up
shaking and covered with sweat, and sit up in bed, but my
wife next to me goes on sleeping, she has a healthy, deep
sleep, the children are asleep too, so in the dark room I
am alone and the whole of my life passes in front of my
eyes, ending up with the greatest misfortune that has ever
befallen me, leaving me without hope that the joy of living
will ever be restored to me.

At the dawn of Independence oh! how differently I
thought of my life – I have always devoted all my energies
to work, and many people, even my own wife, have looked
askance at me, blamed me for not seeing anything outside
work, called me a martinet, but I wasn't doing it to make a
career for myself, only for the good of the community and
this is why I scrupulously observed all directives coming
from above and put them in operation within my limited
scope, because I correctly reasoned that a New Order cannot be built without discipline and a relentless fight for the
New against the Old. I have always been in favour of the
regime and the People's Authority, I have been a member
of the Trades Unions since the day I began work, i.e. for
fifteen years, and although I was struck off the military
register because of my health, in view of my wartime Parti-
san activities I am a member of the Union of Ex-Service-
men and also a member of the Peasant Party.

I have always been socially conscious and now that
I have been removed because of wrongful accusations from

participating in the social, political and economic life of
my country I suffer greatly both as a Pole and a patriot of
the Order for which I once fought, I therefore beg you,
Citizen First Secretary, to consider my appeal as a just
and loving father, the Lord won't forget it and I am sure
you will add this act of mercy and justice to all the benefac-
tions which you have bestowed on the Polish People –
although I have no higher education, you as a good hus-
bandman care for even the smallest blade of corn so that
the grain is never wasted, for we, the sons and daughters
of People's Poland, we are like an enormous field of corn
waving in the wind, and you are the Sun which warms it
and speeds up the process of ripening so that when harvest-
time comes you can cut us for the benefit of the common
weal and so may it come to pass, in the name of the Father
and the Son and the Holy Ghost, Amen.

During the night
I couldn't sleep, I was plagued by restlessness and all kinds
of thoughts, so I went out into the corridor, silence and
calm, only the bracket light is switched on. Wacek Sobieski
is on duty in the men's division tonight, he is a very decent
and pleasant young man, I am on good terms with him, I
like the way he began work in the clinic when he couldn't
get a place at the Medical Faculty, as an ordinary ward
nurse – next year he wants to sit the exams again, he will
certainly pass because he has character and knows what he
wants – his attitude to me is sensible, he didn't make any
difficulties when I told him I couldn't sleep and wanted to
work a little instead, he only enquired whether he should
ask the Duty Medical Officer through the Sister for a

sleeping pill for me, but I told him this was not necessary, so we smoked a cigarette together. He said it was lucky that he hadn't been on duty when that doctor committed suicide, he would have been sacked on the spot, like Wirtek, I don't know if they were right to sack him, as it was not his fault, there was no instruction to keep watch on the bathroom when a patient was bathing, they only tightened up the regulations afterwards, both bathrooms are now locked and opened at specified times on request only, you can only shave between ten and eleven am and at night only one of the three toilets is open, the Ladies', the one with the broken tank. The management have overdone it on this point, because a Gentlemen's is next to the Ladies' and both have windows overlooking the little passage between the Men's and Women's sections, so it is possible to see what the patients are doing inside, one ward sister can watch both lavatories at once. I think that this decision has been taken without giving it much thought and this I call opportunism, not care for the patients, I don't believe the Registrar can have known about this new rule – yesterday and today after television there was a large queue in front of the Ladies'.

But first of all I wanted to note that I had a conversation in the evening with Dr Gwara, it was very strange and I am still wondering what he had in mind when he said, almost precisely in these words: 'Do you know, Mr Konieczny, I quite envy you in a certain sense.' 'What do you mean?' I asked, for I really didn't know what he was talking about, and he then said something like that he was envious of the fact that I have a real and powerful enemy, for the worst thing is to surrender and not do what you want to do, but what others require you to do – this in time becomes a habit and lying becomes your true nature and truth a burden, but one that you cannot quite get rid of – when it nags at you, you don't quite know what to do, you haven't enough courage to admit the truth, yet lying begins to worry you increasingly, you look for various means of stupefying yourself, but nothing can help you, everything gradually becomes worse and worse. 'I know,' he said, 'you don't have it easy, you are suffering in your own way, but at least you are putting up a resistance and a fight for your rights . . . I envy you,' he repeated once more and I then thought that either I didn't understand anything, or else he was feeling guilty towards me and that was why he was using such obscure hints, so I said: 'I should not wish a fate like mine on my worst enemy.' He stopped – we were out for a walk, although the weather was cold and windy – gazed at me strangely and looked so young that I wouldn't have put him at more than thirty, and said: 'I must say, you are a damned decent man, Mr Konieczny, I wish I had colleagues and professors like you, not to speak of all those who are higher up.' I then remembered what he had said about prison and asked: 'Have you also been wronged, Dr Gwara?' 'Oh no,' he smiled, 'I am wronging myself.' I was completely at a loss and asked: 'How can that be?' He waved it aside and said: 'There are so many possibilities, so many.' 'Such as?' I asked and my hands began to shake, I had been feeling increasingly agitated, I don't even remember what else I said because a terrible thought entered my head. 'Excuse me,' I said, 'but I am feeling very restless, I'll have to lie down.' 'Aren't you feeling well?' he asked with assumed interest. 'No,' I answered,

THE APPEAL

'I am all right, just restless,' and I went to lie down and fell asleep so fast and so hard that I had to be woken up for supper. I had no appetite. I must be mistaken, it's impossible that such a man . . . I must have misunderstood him, but when I left the room a while ago I am not sure that he was asleep, his eyes were . . .

Wednesday
I had to interrupt my night's work because Gwara went out of the room to the toilet, but he didn't look like a person who had just woken up, he didn't come up to me, only smiled from the distance, rather strangely, I thought. I have had a headache since the early morning and am feeling very restless.

Thursday
I have a headache and I no longer wish to live, I am trying not to think and to be like a stone, but everything inside me is shaky.

This is the sixth day since I sent off my appeal.

Friday
I am still very agitated and cannot work because my hand keeps slipping away.

Saturday
I had a letter from home, Halina writes that everything is in order – Mickey had a sore throat but is better now, she doesn't even ask when I am returning home, she is probably enjoying her freedom while I am away.

Monday

The Registrar told me during his rounds that I would
return home in a week's time at the latest – I replied that I
still felt very restless and that my mouth was dry. 'This
will pass,' said the Registrar, 'you are fit and I don't want
to see you around here any more.' This decision stunned
me, but I couldn't openly say in the presence of the other
doctors that until receipt of the answer from Citizen First
Secretary my place was here. Everybody congratulated me
that I would be discharged. 'Aren't you lucky?' said
Raphael, because, although he had been expecting to be
discharged soon, he is being kept on here because of the
bad condition of his tonsils.

The Colonel also congratulated me, but Dr Gwara didn't
say a word, only later, during the walk, when I kept away
from the others as I was very depressed, he came up to me
and said: 'Cheer up, Mr Konieczny, why are you worried?
If the letter should come in your absence, Plebanski will at
once forward it to your home address.' 'He may or may
not,' I said, because I felt really depressed. 'What, don't
you trust Dr Plebanski?' he asked, astonished. I felt un-
comfortable because what I had said really sounded tactless
and clumsy, I did not say what was really worrying me. 'It
isn't that,' I said, 'I have always trusted the Registrar and
still do, but I don't trust the post office much, it will be a
letter with an official stamp and there are people everywhere who are interested in other people's affairs, and how
many letters get lost? Here it is different, the address is
official, it isn't as if the letter were to a private individual.'
'One can always register a letter,' said Dr Gwara. 'Yes,
one can,' I said, 'but what guarantee have I that a regis-

tered letter will reach my own hands, I've only got to go out shopping and my brother-in-law will sign for it for me, he might get a special bonus for a letter like that, the Judas. I didn't think that Dr Plebanski would put me in such a difficult position, for apart from the merits of the case I don't feel fit at all and don't feel ready to return home, I am still feeling very restless, my head aches from thinking too much, I am far from healthy, my nerves are frail as cobweb, and *they* are only waiting for me to return home in this depressed state to pounce on me at once, I'm not even sure that I am not watched here by specially planted people.' I said this on purpose to provoke him, but he pretended not to hear or at least not to take in what I had said, he was walking alongside me in silence and strangely thoughtful, until suddenly he became excited.

'You know what, Mr Konieczny,' he exclaimed, 'I have an excellent idea.' 'What?' I asked cautiously, and he then explained: 'I am on good terms with Plebanski, so if a letter from the Central Committee comes for you, I am sure Plebanski won't have any objections and will give me a pass for a day or two, and I can give you my word of honour that I shall personally deliver the letter to you and give it into your own hands – what do you think of that?' I felt a terrible sorrow, because now I knew whom I had to deal with, I felt completely and utterly beaten – for twelve years I have had many agents and spies around me but never one so highly educated, he held me between his treacherous hands and held me tight, cleverly pretending to be a well-wishing friend, and I knew that I could not let on without exposing myself to a terrible danger, perhaps even death, I had to conceal my thoughts and feelings and I felt terribly disappointed that such a nice man could cultivate treason under the guise of friendship and for his own, probably quite considerable benefit, was prepared to deliver me into the hands of his principals who were my enemies. I don't know what was going on in his own conscience when he agreed to disregard all the human and divine laws, for I couldn't believe that he considered me a traitor and agent of a foreign intelligence service, but I couldn't sit in judgment on him, so I said cautiously that I would think about it and thanked him very much for his offer, but I could not put him to so much trouble.

'What trouble?' he interrupted craftily, 'it will be my pleasure, and I shall be able to call on you and perhaps speed up the question of your temporary flat, I have some connections, it's worth trying; I tell you, Mr Konieczny, everything will be all right, you will see.' He spoke so convincingly that for a moment it seemed to me that perhaps I had been mistakenly suspicious of a decent man, I was torn by doubt, because a false accusation is a great sin, I am not one of those who like repaying evil with evil, although I have come out badly from it: such is the world today that neighbourliness is disappearing and men act like wolves towards one another.

I have read a number of times in the *People's Tribune* that conditions are not yet quite normal in our country, there are those who can afford a fridge, a television set, an electric washing machine, even a motor-car and a holiday tour of Bulgaria, Hungary or Jugoslavia, three or even four suits of clothes, even a meal in the evening in an S-category restaurant. I'm not talking of the ones who steal, but those who work honestly in their professions, such as for instance Richard Kuna. I have known him since 1945, he has always been a big man, strong and healthy, he could spend a whole night drinking and enjoying himself, yet in the morning come to work rested, in full possession of his faculties, he went on like this for fifteen years, he earned good money, so he didn't refuse himself any pleasures, he lived comfortably until in April 1964, shortly after I had returned from a stay at the clinic, he died within one hour – he had had a stroke and there was no help for him, and he was just over forty, as I myself am now, he had never complained of heart trouble, never had a day's illness in all the time I had known him, he was hardened to life, but was getting rotten inside and death was growing in him. I don't know why people work so hard and suffer so, perhaps Richard was right when in our Militia days, I remember, he used to say after a few drinks: 'With life, old chap, one must deal as with a woman, grip it tight and f— it right, otherwise you won't get anywhere, you will always be kicked around by everybody.' Perhaps he was right in saying that, but I am not capable of acting like that, I probably have a different nature.

Tuesday
Today is the tenth day since I sent the appeal. I am very restless. The Registrar has been busy, so I have been unable to see him.

Wednesday
I asked to be received by the Registrar, he agreed to see me but was a bit unfriendly, he said at once that he didn't have much time, I felt very nervous but I said calmly:

'I apologize, Mr Registrar, but I wanted to discuss what you were good enough to tell me on Monday.' 'What do you intend to do?' he interrupted at once. 'Get used to the idea,' I said, 'because I think – ' He again did not let me continue: 'Slowly, Mr Konieczny,' he said, 'I am the one to do the thinking who is to be discharged from the clinic and when, that is why I am here. That is the first thing to remember, and secondly, today is Wednesday, so this means' – here he looked at the calendar – 'that next Wednesday you will take the train for home, I have told you already that you are well and that I don't want to see you around here any more.' 'But the point is, Mr Registrar,' I said, 'that I am not well.' 'What?' exclaimed the Registrar and got quite red in the face, 'You aren't well? Perhaps you would like to be sent to Tworki for further treatment, because we can't help you any more here for the time being, we could do that, you could even go there tomorrow by train, under escort of course.'

When I heard this I felt as if somebody had hit me on the head, I felt completely empty inside. 'Surely you don't wish to destroy me, Mr Registrar, you don't want to bury me alive,' I said, 'I have been feeling my nerves very badly lately, and in addition there is the appeal you know about.' 'Mr Konieczny,' said the Registrar, 'let's talk sensibly, shall we? I know very well what makes you anxious, I understand you, don't interrupt me, please, I understand your anxiety so well that I've agreed to Dr Gwara's suggestion, although you must realize that it does not conform to the customs of this clinic that a patient should play postman instead of undergoing treatment, but in this instance, because I understand you, I'll shut my eyes to the rules, I'll make an exception and if the letter from the Central Committee should come in your absence, Dr Gwara will personally deliver it to you. I think this is all I can do for you, and in any case you cannot expect me to indulge you and calmly listen to your blackmail about your health, *you are well* and as I have already said, next Wednesday you will leave here. I hope you understand me?' 'Yes, Mr Registrar,' I said, 'I can see that the enemy's hand is tightening the chain around my neck.' The Registrar looked at me askance: 'What did you say?' 'I said what I know, Mr Registrar,' I replied. 'And what does that mean?' he asked, 'perhaps you will express yourself more clearly.' 'I am expressing myself quite clearly, Mr Registrar,' I said, 'only I cannot speak about everything I know and think.' 'Mr Konieczny,' said the Registrar, 'I am going to advise you not as a doctor but as a friend: if you insist on thinking, do so, but try hard not to harm yourself, we doctors are unfortunately not omnipotent, we have tried to restore your shaken mental equilibrium, that's all, full stop, we cannot do anything more for you, you yourself must watch your equilibrium, and first of all say goodbye, once and for all, to all your delusions about the hostile hand of the enemy and so on and so forth. Try to think calmly about it all.' 'Yes, Mr Registrar,' I said, 'I know that you wish me well.' 'I hope you do,' he replied, 'I have trust in your good sense, Mr Konieczny.'

I left his office obediently, but quite depressed, for life didn't seem to me to be worth living any more, I would have preferred to be watched, as before, by pairs or threes of low-grade spies snooping on me and aping me, than to have one very powerful agent preparing a noose for me with one hand while hypocritically offering friendly services with the other. I felt helpless in these circumstances and completely alone, because it is not within my competence to convince the Registrar of the bad faith of his friend, he would rather believe a man on the same level of education as himself than someone like me who only finished six classes of primary school, although afterwards, whenever I had an opportunity, I absorbed all the learning available to me and spared no efforts and sacrifices in that line. I didn't even wonder at the Registrar's attitude and didn't resent it, because I understood that it is easier for him to find a common language with the other man, I only very much regretted that such a clever and generous man had succumbed to one who is also clever but perverse. Probably generosity of spirit does not pay, it must have weak foundations.

I lay down, although I was plagued by restlessness – my Judas wasn't there, he must have gone for a walk, so I thought how terribly difficult it is in this world to wield power responsibly, for a man who is honest and pure as the driven snow is helpless when faced with deceit, dark machinations and plots. I now understand the saints who withdrew from men and the world in order to live out their lives in a locked cell or in the desert – only I ask, what is to happen to people like myself, innocently persecuted and pushed to the margin of life, what can the people and the nation do if there are no just men at the top, if it is the devils who hold the power, who cling to it and say to the nation: 'We shall make angels of you,' yet behave in such a way and oppress people so that the devil's own brew comes of it. Where is there any help or salvation? It is idle to call for help, no one will hear, and even if they did they wouldn't understand . . .

Thursday
My God, my God, why have you forsaken me?

Friday
I don't want to think about it but I can't stop myself from thinking.

Saturday
The fourteenth day since I sent my appeal to the Citizen First Secretary of the Central Committee of the Polish United Workers' Party, Warsaw. I pray that the answer, my only salvation, shall come in time.

Sunday
As the date is approaching on which, on the instructions of the Director, Citizen Registrar Dr Stefan Plebanski, I have to leave this clinic, I feel it my duty to inform you, Citizen First Secretary, that on Saturday at five pm the agent entrusted by the Counter-intelligence with watching me and confounding my plans came into the open, which means that his principals must feel sufficiently strong and sure of themselves to start an open offensive. At the above-mentioned time Dr Matthew Gwara, lecturer at T University, sitting on his bed in my presence, produced from his brief-case a folder with documents, looked cursorily through them, then before my very eyes shamelessly began to tear them up and put the torn ones to one side, looking at me strangely all the time. I was sitting nearby, next to my bed,

I was mesmerized as if by the stare of a poisonous snake, for I swear, although I have told Dr Gwara a lot of facts about my life, considering him a friend and an honest person, I have never mentioned to him that in 1955 I destroyed the development plans for the Cane-Panel and Pre-Fabricated One-Family House factory at Wilkasy. While he was tearing up these papers, so giving me to understand that he knew everything relating to all the circumstances of my former activities, I did not ask him any questions for, as I have mentioned, I was completely numb with shock.

He spoke first and said: 'You probably can't even guess, Mr Konieczny, what part you have played in my decision to tear up and destroy this unfinished essay.' 'I don't understand,' I said softly, because my throat was numb too and terribly dry, and then, still busily tearing up the papers, which were identical to mine, he said: 'You gave me an example that it is worth while not to lie, even at the risk of a lot of unpleasantness, I owe you a lot, Mr Konieczny,' and as I still did not say anything, but only breathed heavily, that accursed Judas asked hypocritically: 'Aren't you feeling well, Mr Konieczny?' I somehow managed to answer: 'I am feeling all right, only very restless, excuse me Dr Gwara, but I must go for a walk, perhaps that will help me,' and I went out into the corridor.

I now communicate this fact to you, Citizen First Secretary, so that you may know that Citizen Dr Matthew Gwara, a socioligist by profession, is an important agent of the Counter-intelligence and that in view of the anti-Party activities of that Office, you should draw the right conclusions for the defence of legality.

THE APPEAL

In the event of my sudden death, I consider Dr Matthew Gwara to be its perpetrator and guilty of it.

Monday
No new signs on his part, but I am maintaining increased vigilance, although I know now that there is no hope for me, God has forsaken me and so has everybody else.

Tuesday
A great day has come, a great moment, I am emerging from a dark abyss into the brightly lit world! A little while ago postman Golebiowski, whom I know well because both during my previous and my present stay here he has paid me out money orders, stopped me on the stairs when I was going for a walk and said: 'Ho, ho! Mr Konieczny, I have an important letter for you, from very, very high up, almost from Heaven itself.' I must have grown very pale, for darkness had filled my head and my heart, and the postman must have been frightened by my appearance, because he grabbed me by the elbow and said: 'Christ Almighty, why are you so pale? I am not pulling your leg, on my honour I am not – there is a letter for you from the CC.' I had already come round. 'Show it to me,' I said, 'let me see it with my own eyes.' He hesitated a little, but reached into his bag. 'All right,' he said, 'for you I'll make an exception, you know very well, Mr Konieczny, that I am not allowed to hand the patients their correspondence directly, it's not my fault.' 'I know, I know,' I said, 'it will be quite enough if I can see it.'

A man lost in a terrible desert and dying of thirst, when he sees a wonderful oasis, or a castaway on a boundless ocean who sees rescue on the horizon, must feel what I felt when I saw an envelope in Golebiowski's hands with, printed in its left corner, 'Central Committee of the PUWP'. 'I didn't know, Mr Konieczny,' said the postman, 'that you had connections with such high office.' 'This is justice, Mr Golebiowski,' I replied and I could not finish my sentence I was so overcome with happiness, but now I am calm and waiting patiently to be summoned by the Registrar, to receive the Highest Word, which will bring me Justice at last.

It is a dull day today, grey skies, rain is beginning to fall, but inside me everything is bright as for a Mayday service, my twelve years of hell on earth have come to an end, my unmasked enemies have been forced to capitulate and each citizen of this country will be clearly told that I am innocent and pure as the driven snow, thanks be to you, God Almighty, for having heard my prayers and thanks be to you, Citizen First Secretary, from the depths of my heart I thank you and promise you solemnly that I shall strive with all my strength to serve People's Poland and the New Order selflessly and efficiently, and may this come to pass in the name of the Father, the Son and the Holy Ghost, Amen.

*

Here Marian Konieczny's notes end.

That day, Dr Plebanski was holding a two-hour seminar for young psychiatrists devoted to Study for Perfecting the Efficiency of the Medical Team, so that it was only after dinner at about two pm that he summoned Konieczny.

'Well now, Mr Konieczny,' he called from behind his

desk as Konieczny came in, 'you are lucky, your waiting is over. Please be seated and read this letter calmly, I must say that I did not expect your case to be considered so quickly, I congratulate you.'

But when Konieczny was handed the letter he could not read it: he was long-sighted and had forgotten his glasses, and besides, his hands were shaking.

'Shall I read it?' asked Plebanski helpfully.

'If you would be so kind, Mr Registrar,' said Konieczny, 'I left my glasses behind by mistake.'

He half-closed his eyes to hear better; he was sitting upright, his face turned towards the Registrar. Plebanski began to read slowly and distinctly. The letter was short. In concise, official terms it stated quite clearly that according to the information collected at the personal instruction of Citizen First Secretary, there had never been any accusations against the integrity of Citizen Marian Konieczny, therefore all the doubts and fears set forth in the Citizen's appeal of such and such a date must be the result of a misunderstanding and could not become the subject of any further investigations.

Konieczny was listening completely immobile; his eyes were still closed and he did not open them when Plebanski finished reading and put the letter on the desk.

'Well, Mr Konieczny!' he said. 'Here you have in writing everything you wanted to hear. One might say that after a long voyage you have at last reached a quiet haven.'

Only then did Konieczny lift his eyelids. The gaze of his glassy, slightly faded eyes fell on the Registrar.

'You have won, Mr Registrar,' he said softly.

To which Plebanski replied:

'It is mostly your victory, maybe I have played a small part in it but it's mostly yours.'

'You have buried me,' said Konieczy.

Plebanski started.

'What did you say?'

'You have buried me. You have arranged all this very cleverly and falsified the letter.'

Plebanski reddened.

'What?' he exclaimed. 'What are you talking about? How dare you speak to me like that! Hysteria and delusions again, I'll beat them out of your head. What *do* you mean?'

'You have the power to do anything,' said Konieczny softly.

This almost humble admission quietened Plebanski somewhat.

'I am glad you believe so. But what are you thinking about? What is the matter with you? Just consider, dear Mr Konieczny. Here you have in black and white a statement, from the most competent person, that you are blameless, so what are you up to now, has happiness made you confused?'

'You have sold me, Judas,' said Konieczny and rose heavily from his chair, putting both his palms on the desk. 'You and the other fellow, you have both made a pact to destroy me. How much did you get? Five, ten thousand, perhaps more? Don't interrupt me, I am talking now and I know what I am saying when I tell you that I consider this scrap of paper to be a falsification, or else the First Secretary has never even looked at my appeal, because agents of the Counter-intelligence penetrated into his nearest surroundings and you gave them warning in time. I understand everything, you planned it a long time ago, for such were your orders, should I refuse to give in. You have prepared a shameful end for me, yet I trusted you boundlessly, as my own father. Don't be afraid, I shall not curse you, but in the hour of your death may my terrible misfortune fall heavily on your head.'

A long moment passed before Dr Plebanski could speak. Then he said:

' Unfortunately you were right, Mr Konieczny, you cannot return home for the time being. Nothing doing, you must stay with us, I cannot at present tell you for how long. I am very disappointed in you, Mr Konieczny. You may now return to your room.'

Without a word, Konieczny obediently turned to go, but stopped in the doorway and turned round.

'You have buried me alive, Judas,' he said in accents of great suffering and sorrow.

Having said this he left the office and, as the corridor was full of patients and noise, took refuge in the lavatory, the third one without a window, the one always locked at night.

There he felt void, emptied of everything, covered with only a fine layer of skin, and it was as if this skin were turned inside out, dead on the outside but extra-sensitive to his inner emptiness. He was listening to the nerve-ends of this skin strangely turned inside-out, receiving only the sensation of a deepening vacuum, until he began to realize that something was happening inside him, something inconceivable and frightening, spreading like the growing darkness of night, or perhaps the reverse, like the brightening

light of day. He was being filled with an enormous movement, a swirl like a cosmic vortex – yes, yes! attentive and
quiet he now knew that the cosmos has entered his emptiness, the boundless and infinite cosmos, to continue inside
him its eternal movement and rush towards the unknown.
Contrary to the inadequate knowledge he had about the
revolutions of heavenly bodies, the solar systems circling in
space within and together with powerful galaxies were now
circling within the vacuum bounded by his skin, not in dead
silence but with a terrible creaking, moaning and groaning.
He listened attentively with the nerve-ends of his inside-
out skin to these sounds, amongst which he distinctly recognized his own groans, intensified by the fever of typhoid, the
plaintive weeping of a child over the body of a squirrel,
some distant shots from an automatic pistol, perhaps even
the rustlings of a forest of high trees, the cracking of dry
twigs and the murmur of leaves; listening intently he
nodded his head in time to the sound of the creaks, groans,
laments and tremors, as if checking them carefully and having recognized them, tenderly accepting them, until at last,
feeling very tired and sleepy, he sat down on the lavatory
seat and rested his head on his hands; and then silence
filled him and surrounded him as, still with his head on his
hands, hunching his back, he began to cry loudly.

A little later the small, pretty brunette, Sister Irena,
worried by Konieczny's disappearance, found him there and
began to comfort him with maternal tenderness like a small
child but he did not recognize her, refused to get up, did
not allow her to pull his hands from around his head, only
cried and cried.